CATRIONA McCUAIG

HEART OF DARKNESS

Complete and Unabridged

LINFORD
Leicester

First published in Great Britain in 2009

First Linford Edition
published 2010

British Library CIP Data

McCuaig, Catriona.
  Heart of darkness.- -
(Linford romance library)
1. Great Britain- -History- -Henry VIII,
1509 – 1547- -Fiction.
2. Love stories 3. Large type books.
I. Title II. Series
813.6–dc22

ISBN 978–1–44480–149–1

Published by
F. A. Thorpe (Publishing)
Anstey, Leicestershire

Set by Words & Graphics Ltd.
Anstey, Leicestershire
Printed and bound in Great Britain by
T. J. International Ltd., Padstow, Cornwall

This book is printed on acid-free paper

1

Had it not been for the mouse in the larder, Meg Makepeace would never have been anywhere near the graveyard that morning, and in that case she would not have been unfortunate enough to discover the body.

When her mother died, Meg had begun to help her sister-in-law with the running of the household and they had worked well together until Elizabeth's untimely death in childbirth two years ago. Meg had gladly stepped into the breach then, caring for her father, Ben Makepeace, as well as attending to the grieving widower and his orphaned children, with the aid of one small maid. This state of affairs might have gone on for years had her brother not decided to marry again, this time to a woman who was vastly different in temperament from his poor lost Bess.

Meg, prepared to welcome Margery Peacock into the family with a cheerful heart, had been taken aback by the way in which she'd been elbowed aside by Adam's bossy new wife.

'She's the mistress of the house, now,' Ben said, when appealed to. 'You've got to allow her a bit of leeway, gal. Besides, she's used to running a household, what with her being married before. You've managed very well since Bess and your poor mother died, God rest their souls, and we're grateful, but now you can sit back a bit. Why not take it easy? You'll be married yourself soon enough, I dare say; you don't want to waste what's left of your girlhood scrubbing floors and scouring pots.'

But Margery obviously thought otherwise. Despite the fact that she had brought two more maids with her from her old home, she treated Meg like a hired hand, and a none too satisfactory one, at that. For her part, Meg deeply resented the fact that everything in the kitchen was rearranged by the household's new mistress, and she said as much to her brother. He wasn't sympathetic.

'Really, Meg! How do you think Margery feels when you keep saying Mumma did this, and Mumma did that? She's my wife. Of course she wants things done in her own way.'

'Bess didn't.'

Adam's expression softened for a moment, remembering. 'That was then. This is now. Just try to keep the peace, Meggie, for Dad's sake if nothing else. You know how he hates squabbling.'

So Meg did her best, and when Margery threw out a pewter vase that had been a favourite of Meg's mother, saying that she wouldn't have a lot of clutter in her house, the girl quietly retrieved it from the midden where it had landed and smuggled it up to her room.

This morning, though, matters had come to a head. Going into the larder, Meg had moved a box aside and in doing so disturbed a small field mouse which had been lurking at the back of the shelf. The terrified creature ran down her arm and she let out a piercing scream, staggering backwards in her haste to get out of the way. It was pure bad luck that she cannoned into a keg of flour, knocking it over and spilling the contents. Margery was at her side in a trice, adding her voice to the din.

'Now see what you've done, you stupid girl! All that good flour wasted! Do you think I'm made of money?'

Shock made Meg respond more rudely than she would otherwise have done.

'It's your own stupid fault, Margery! If you weren't always moving things away from their proper place, I wouldn't have tripped over the flour bin. Why can't you leave things where they belong?'

Margery raised a hand to deliver a slap, as Meg side-stepped nimbly. 'How dare you speak to me like that, you wicked girl! I'll make you pay for this, you see if I don't!'

When any of the maids had an accident, the result of carelessness, the new Mistress Makepeace made a habit of deducting a groat or two from their meagre wages, but surely she wouldn't dare to try to extract money from the daughter of the house? Or did the woman mean to make her young sister-in-law pay in some other way? Probably both, Meg reflected. Well, she might as well be hung for a sheep as a lamb!

'I'm going out, Margery. I'll see you later.'

'What? You'll do no such thing! If you know what's good for you you'll get down on your knees and clear up this mess you've made. Come back here, I say!' But she was talking to thin air. Meg was gone.

Meg was out of the yard and halfway up the lane before she began to calm down. Her bosom heaving, she pulled off the white cap covering her soft hair to let the cooling breeze reach her brow. What a fool she'd been to let herself get in such a state! The trouble was, there was no reasoning with the woman.

She wondered anew what had attracted her brother to the officious Mistress Peacock. She had said as much to her father, after the first time Adam had brought his intended bride home. Margery had looked around the house as if she owned the place, not seeing it as the comfortable family home it was, but as a repository of all her fancy belongings, handed down in the family of the late Master Peacock.

Meg would never forget those first words. 'Hmm, well, it's small, but 'twill have to do. My oak chest will look well enough there, under the window, and we'll get rid of some of those old fashioned chairs to make room for mine.' Meg had been about to protest when she'd caught sight of the expression on her father's face. 'Let it be,' he seemed to be saying, 'We'll sort it out later.'

And so he had. 'Every woman has a right to have her own things about her, gal. Never fear, your mother's things shan't be thrown away. We'll put them in the old loft and Margery will be none the wiser. They'll come into their own again some day.'

Meanwhile, Meg had done her best to be agreeable, for Adam's sake. She hadn't done too badly until now, but resentment had been building up inside her, culminating in this morning's outburst.

She was now on her way to the old Norman church. Not to go quietly inside to pray, because she wasn't ready to let go of her anger yet, but to visit her mother's grave in the churchyard. She always found peace there, while she poured out her heart to Kate Makepeace, just as she had done as a child, bringing her childish woes to her mother, who had always seemed ready to listen and to soothe.

Perhaps it was silly, talking to someone who was cold clay, lying six feet under the sod; Meg knew that at the back of her mind. Yet, when she did so, it always seemed that her mother's spirit was hovering somewhere nearby, watching her only daughter with love and concern. Whatever the truth of the matter, there was comfort to be found here.

She knelt down, carefully arranging the spring flowers she had picked in the lane, and then she sat back on her heels, trying to marshal her thoughts. The graveyard was beautiful at this time of year, with new grass springing up everywhere, and rosy-tipped daisies pushing their way towards the sun. A butterfly flew close to Meg's shoulder and darted away again, and in the distance a wood dove could be heard, calling for a mate. A feeling of wellbeing washed over her. She had been right to come.

Still on her knees, she wriggled over to the next mound, which covered the earthly remains of Adam's first wife, Bess, who slept there with her new born babe in her arms and her five-year-old daughter at her side.

'I'll watch out for your Ned,' Meg promised, wondering if Bess somehow knew about the trouble they were having with the little boy. His grandfather was inclined to make excuses for him, saying that the lad missed his mother, and all would come right in time, but how could one know the real cause of his sulks and stubbornness? Some people were born with a certain temperament and not all the mothering in the world could make a difference.

It certainly hadn't helped that Margery had brought her young son with her to put Ned's nose out of joint. Young Hugh Peacock was a nice enough child, but the very fact of his being in the house meant a certain rivalry between the boys, and naturally enough his mother took his side when things went wrong.

Meg sighed, and hauled herself to her feet. While she was here she might as well go to the older part of the graveyard, where her mother's people were buried in the shadow of the yew trees.

Rounding the corner, she was amazed to see a man lying in the grass. A scythe had been abandoned on the ground a few feet away. A funny time to take a nap, she thought, this early in the day, and who on earth was it? He was much taller than old Josh, whose regular work it was to keep the graveyard in good trim.

Why, only yesterday she had heard the old fellow grumbling to her father about how much work there was for one man, and how the priest was too miserly to part with the few pennies it would cost to get a boy to share the load.

Should she turn away before he realised anyone was there? She was a kind girl, and had no wish to cause embarrassment. Common sense took over. She had every right to be here.

She coughed tentatively, giving the fellow a chance to pull himself together before she came closer, but he didn't stir. She coughed again, but still there was no response.

Growing bolder now, she came level with the reclining figure, and it was then she realised that she was looking at a corpse.

2

Adam makepeace and his father were hard at work in the forge, where they had been since shortly after dawn. As yet there were no horses waiting to be shod, but the two men had plenty of other tasks to be getting on with. Adam was fashioning shoes of various sizes, mostly large ones meant for plough horses, a process which would save time when they were needed, later on. Ben was seeing to various items which had been brought in for repair by people from round about.

'What was all that about this morning?' he enquired, frowning at a fishing spear which had somehow got bent out of shape. 'Raised voices!'

'Women's arguments, I s'pose. Just a fuss about nothing.' Adam shrugged.

'Didn't sound like nothing to me, boy! Didn't I see your sister racing off like the seven devils was at her heels?'

'They'll get over it, whatever it was. Anyway, I've told our Meg she'll have to give way to Margery when it comes to things in the house. She's my wife, Dad; she's due her rights.'

'True enough, boy, but what about your sister? This is her home. She was born here. Doesn't she have rights, too?'

Adam sighed. 'What that girl needs is a home of her own. Once she's married she can throw her weight around as much as she likes, and leave me in peace. I can't be doing with women sniping at each other. Why can't they get along peaceable like, same as you and me?'

'Seems to me your Margery's a bit too much on edge these days,' Ben persisted. 'Not in the family way, is she?'

'Not that I know of, Dad. No, it's this business of young Hugh, see?'

'Ah! Been at you again, has she?'

Adam nodded. 'She wants me to take

her boy on as an apprentice when he's old enough, and I've said no.'

'And quite right, too! There've been Makepeaces here as far back as anyone can remember, and there'll be Makepeaces here long after we're gone. Hugh's a good enough lad, but he's not of our blood, boy. It's your young Ned who'll inherit when the time comes, as is right and proper.'

'Yes, Ned.' Adam sniffed, wiping his nose on the back of his hand, but Ned was no more likely to make a good blacksmith than the man in the moon, and, young as he was, Margery knew it, and she wasn't backward in making her views plain.

Ben knew what his son was thinking. 'I admit it's a bit of a drawback he's mortal afraid of horses, but he's young yet. He'll grow out of that.'

'And if he doesn't.'

'Then there's plenty more work for a good blacksmith to do. Anyway, you'll get more sons from Margery, I don't doubt. No need to worry yet.'

'That don't settle the problem of Hugh Peacock.'

'Never you mind about that. I've a bit put by, enough to pay his indentures so's he can learn a good trade somewhere else. Let him be a saddler, say, or a cooper. Any mother would be proud to see her son set up like that.'

'Try telling that to Margery,' Adam said gloomily. 'One reason she wants him apprenticed to me is so she can keep her eye on him here.'

'Under her thumb, more like, and that's no good for a growing boy.'

'She's afraid he'd be treated badly, working for some strict master.'

'And what harm would the odd whipping do?' Ben demanded. 'Teach him how to get on in the world. We've all got to learn, and treating a boy too soft does him no favours. And that's another reason for not taking him on here. Give him a cuff round the ear, richly deserved, and Margery'd be on her high horse, kissing him better. No, lad; just you stick to your guns. It'll be worth it in the long run.'

Both men bent to their work, and nothing more was said for a considerable time. The sound of hammering filled the forge. As far as father and son were concerned, it was a day like any other.

Adam Makepeace, who was a man in his prime, was the very picture of a village blacksmith; tall, muscular, genial. Ben, too, had been a handsome fellow in his day, but he was less straight-backed than his son, and inclined to limp when the wind was in the east. Long years of bending over the anvil had affected him, and every once in a while what afflicted him was known as the blacksmiths' strike, when his muscles seized up and he had to take to his bed for a day.

It was then that he appreciated his daughter most, lying face down under the weight of the hot, wet cloths she brought him. Nothing else seemed to help as well.

Thinking about Meg must have made

him conjure her up, for suddenly there she was, standing in the entrance to the forge, in a state of some agitation.

Adam's jaw dropped. His sister's white apron was spattered with what looked like blood. Well aware of what had taken place earlier that morning he immediately connected her appearance with her disagreement with Margery. Surely they hadn't come to blows? His wife was quick tempered, but not inclined to violence, other than to deliver a well deserved clip round the ear to the maids or the children. Could she have thrown something at Meg?

Ben took in the situation right away. 'Are you all right, gal? You look a bit peaky. And what's all that on your hem?'

'I'm all right, Dad,' she muttered, swaying as she spoke.

'Don't look like it to me! Here, come and sit down, before you fall down!' He led her to a bench and pushed her head down between her knees. After a moment she sat up, still looking wan.

'Now, what's happened here? You look white as a ghost, my girl! Seen something you hadn't oughta?'

She nodded. 'There's a body in the graveyard, Dad.'

Adam let out a great guffaw. 'Pull the other leg, Meg, it's got bells on! What else would there be in the graveyard but bodies, eh?'

Ben frowned at him. 'Let the girl tell her story, boy! Can't you see she's not joking?'

Meg swallowed hard. 'I went to Mumma's grave, see. I was feeling out of sorts and I thought it'd make me feel better. I talk to her sometimes, you know, and tell her what's troubling me. It comforts me.' She glanced at Adam out of the corner of her eye, willing him not to laugh at her again.

'Get on with it, then,' Ben encouraged.

'Well, I wasn't ready to come home yet, so I thought I'd go and pay a visit to the old folk, round the corner by the yews.'

Ben nodded. His own parents and

grandparents were buried there, and he sometimes wandered in that direction himself, to make sure that everything was neat and tidy as it should be.

'There was a man lying in the grass, Dad. I thought at first he was sleeping, but he didn't answer when I called out so I went a bit closer, in case he was taken ill and needed help. Then I saw that he was dead!'

Her voice rose and Adam was quick to interrupt. He had no patience with weeping women.

'Probably his heart gave out, then,' he surmised.

Meg's eyes filled with tears. 'His throat was cut. I reached down and rolled him over and it was all blood and . . . ' She retched uselessly. She had lost her breakfast before she ever left the churchyard and there was nothing left in her stomach now.

'Why'd you do that?' Adam demanded. 'You'd no call to go interfering with dead bodies, my girl. None of your business, was it?'

'I didn't know he was dead then, did I? When I touched him he was still warm. I thought to help him, if I could.'

Ben and Adam exchanged glances. Fortunately Meg did not see this.

'Let's get this straight, then,' Ben said. 'You found this chap lying in the grass, face down. You thought at first he was sleeping.'

'Yes.'

'Funny place to take a nap, then. If a chap wanted a few minutes' peace, better to settle under the shade of them yews, I'd have said.'

'How was I supposed to know what he was up to?'

'True. And was he all alone? Did you see anyone else about?'

'No, Dad, or I wouldn't have done what I did.'

Ben nodded. 'Strikes me we've got a murder on our hands, then. Have you fetched Tom Woodcock?'

Meg shook her head. 'I went to the church first, looking for the priest. I mean, you're supposed to have a priest when someone dies, aren't you? But there was nobody there, so then I went to Tom's cottage, but he wasn't there either. I didn't know what else to do, so I came home.'

'Well, Tom will have to be told, him being the constable. Finish up what you're doing, Adam, and go and hunt him down. I'll get up to the church and keep watch over the corpse until Tom or the priest get there. And you'd better go indoors first, and let your wife know what's up.'

'She doesn't need to know my every move,' Adam grumbled, resentment welling up inside him at being told what to do, like a callow boy.

'Maybe not,' his father agreed, 'but what if a customer comes looking, expecting to find us here, same as usual? What's the woman supposed to say then, eh? No call to make her look foolish in front of strangers! Besides, look at your sister, struck all of a heap! She wants putting to bed after all she's been through!'

Margery's eyes widened when she took in the spectacle of Meg, escorted by Adam, and apparently speechless. 'What have you been and done now, then, Meg Makepeace? And what's that all over your clean apron?'

'It's blood!' Adam snapped, 'and before you ask, no, it's not hers. She came across a corpse up at the churchyard. It's some chap with his throat cut. I just came to let you know that Dad and I'll be gone for a while, that's all.'

'I don't know if that'll ever come clean,' Margery grumbled. 'Take if off and give it to me, and I'll put it to soak. You can give it a good rub later.'

'Did you not hear what I said, woman? There's been a murder, and I have to go and see about it.'

The news seemed to penetrate at last, as his wife turned pale and began to shake.

'Murder? In Meppershall? Surely not.'

'It's murder, all right, and Meg was

witness to it, or pretty near. Dad says she's to go to bed for the rest of the day and you're to see that she does as she's told.'

Margery nodded, and put out her hand for the spoiled apron. Meg removed it and handed it to her.

3

Ben made his way to the church, mulling things over as he went. He had seen death in plenty throughout his life, and the prospect of seeing a corpse held no terrors for him. It was something else that worried him, and he was thankful that the implications seemed to have passed Meg by. That was one good thing about shock; it protected you from the worst when something bad happened.

She'd said the body was still warm when she touched it, and she managed to get blood all over herself when she'd turned it over. The chap must have been newly dead, and seeing as he'd been dispatched from this world by some other man, or men, why then, the killer must have been close by, perhaps even watching Meg while she made her gruesome discovery. The girl could have been in deadly danger in that case; still was, perhaps, if the murderer couldn't be sure that he hadn't been seen.

'And another thing,' Ben muttered, not realising that he'd spoken aloud, 'how come she didn't hear nothing?' Sounds of a scuffle, perhaps, or a cry for help. But no, she'd mentioned nothing like that. It might be she'd remember something later, when she'd had time to simmer down a bit.

Instead of going straight to where the corpse was supposed to be, he decided to try to trace his daughter's footsteps. First he went to his wife's grave, where he stood for a moment, muttering a quiet prayer. He glanced over at the grassy mound which covered his daughter-in-law and two grandchildren.

He'd been fond of young Bess. It was a shame she'd been taken from them too soon but there, what was the point in questioning the ways of God? No doubt He had His reasons, hard though it was for us poor souls down here on earth to fathom. One thing was certain, it wasn't the good Lord who had willed the death of whoever that was lying here with his throat slashed. That had to do with the man and the Devil.

He rounded the corner and there, as Meg had said, the man lay, with his limbs all awry, like a discarded doll. That was Meg's doing, of course. She had rolled him over and he'd flopped on to his back, and she'd started back in alarm and left him in that position.

Ben stared at the dead man. It was nobody he knew. Being a blacksmith, Ben knew everyone for miles around. Sooner or later they all came to the forge, for one reason or another. This was a stranger. He'd been a tall, well set up man, in his thirties, perhaps. Decently dressed, so not a vagrant. He wore a good leather purse at his belt; Ben bent down and unfastened it. It contained a few coins and nothing else. The motive wasn't robbery, then, not unless the murderer had been disturbed by Meg's coming and had run off before he had time to finish the job.

Seeing nothing else of interest, Ben turned his attention to the scythe, which was lying on the grass some distance away. 'Better not touch that,' he told himself, 'or Tom Woodcock'll give me what for.' There was no doubt in his mind that this was the murder weapon, with blood all over the blade. He peered closer, hoping to identify the tool. It could well be one of his own making, which was likely to be if it belonged here in the hamlet.

He wished that the constable would hurry up and get here, so they could discuss the possibilities. It wasn't often that something important happened to break the monotony of the daily round, and although he wouldn't wish the poor chap any harm he was dead now, and that was that.

What everyone would want to know was how a complete stranger happened to be working here in the churchyard. And seeing as he was a stranger, why would anyone want to kill him? Unless, of course, he hadn't been working here at all. Someone else might have been labouring here, and, finding himself the victim of an attack by a madman, managed to swing the scythe to protect himself.

Ben's train of thought was interrupted by the arrival of Adam, accompanied by the constable.

'You took your time!' he said, by way of greeting. Woodcock ignored this sally. He had known Ben Makepeace all his life, having grown up alongside Adam, and he knew how to take him.

'So what's been going on here?' he demanded, matching the older man's gruff tone.

'The grim reaper's been at it again,' Ben told him, chuckling at his own wit.

'So I see. Do you happen to recognise this scythe, then? Is it one of your own making?'

'Mebbe, mebbe not. Tis hard to tell when it's covered in blood like this.'

Tom grunted, and walked over to look at the victim. 'Nobody I know,' he admitted. 'Must have been a stranger, passing through.'

Adam chortled. 'And so he just stopped off here in time to get himself murdered? Nothing to do with us, then. Let's say he was followed by someone known to him, someone with a grudge against him, another foreigner.'

By this he meant not a Frenchman, or a Spaniard, but a man from outside the county. People were always suspicious of foreigners. This was a means of protection, dating from the olden times, when strangers arriving without warning were likely to have ulterior motives, like carrying off your livestock, or worse, your daughters. In those rare cases where murder or mayhem occurred it was always more satisfactory to have suspicion fall on an outsider.

Tom shook his head slowly. 'Now is that likely, Adam? Think about it, man. Say you mean to kill someone like this chap, who may have done you a wrong. You know he means to make a journey, so you decide to follow him. If you can kill him far away from home, nobody will suspect you, and in fact the deed may not even become known to the folk in your own place.'

'Well, what's wrong with that, then? Makes good sense to me.'

'Ah, but what about the murder weapon, eh? All well and good if you intend to stab him or garrotte him, but a scythe? You don't go trotting along the highways and byways carrying one of them! It wouldn't be my choice of a weapon anyhow. No. I say that someone local is behind this, and the sooner we find out who this tool belongs to, the better twill be.'

Ben sniffed. 'What I think is, somebody was working here in the churchyard, all proper, like, when this stranger comes up and attacks him. Wants to rob him, let's say.'

'It would be a brave man who'd attack a chap flinging a scythe about,' Adam grumbled.

'Never you mind that, boy! He could have crept up behind him, tackled him, perhaps, and got him on the ground.

Then the labourer chap fights back, and the robber gets it in the neck. And that's not so unlikely as you might think,' he went on, seeing Adam's look of disbelief. 'Scythes is dangerous things. It's hard to learn how to use one of them. Why, I've seen a youngster get one wrapped around his ankles before now.'

Tom scratched his head. 'I'll have to speak to the priest, of course, but if what you think is true, Ben, then the killer — by accident or design — must be whoever was working here this morning. And that, my friend, is old Josh Palmer!'

'Oh!' Ben said. He had known Josh all his life, a decent enough fellow, but inclined to be a bit harum scarum in his youth. He would hate to see the old man swinging from the gallows, all as a result of his own half-baked theories as to what might have taken place here this morning.

He stood silently by while Tom investigated the victim's money pouch.

No point in mentioning that he'd already done that; the constable might construe it as interference. Perhaps he shouldn't have meddled, but there, no harm had been done. It wasn't as if he'd concealed evidence.

'He's lying in a funny sort of way,' Tom said now. 'All sprawled out like that. You'd think if he fell backwards he'd look different somehow, not with one arm sort of doubled back under.'

Ben cleared his throat. 'Well, now, that would be on account of my Meg having rolled him over.'

'What? That was a fool thing to do, if you like! There might have been something to see that we've missed now. Meg should have let well alone, and I'll tell her so when I see her.'

'There's no call for you to talk like that, Tom Woodcock! How was she to know the chap was dead? She thought he'd been struck down with apoplexy or the like and mebbe there was something she could do. She wasn't to know he was past help, not till she got him on his back and saw all that blood spilling out from under his chin.'

'Well, I daresay she meant well, but I'll still have to talk to her. She must have heard or seen something, even if she didn't realise it at the time. Best I do it right away, before it fades from her mind.'

Fades from her mind! Ben thought. Not likely! 'Then just you be careful how you go about it, my lad!' he grunted. 'The poor girl's had a terrible shock. No need for you to go making her feel worse. She meant no harm.'

Tom's face wore a sheepish grin as he answered this remark. 'I'd never do anything to hurt your Meg, Ben. Have no fear of that.'

4

An interesting little tableau had formed in the kitchen of the Makepeace house when young Ned had rushed in to say that Tom Woodcock was on his way, marching up the lane at that very moment. Adam and Ben followed close on his heels, still wearing their leather aprons, and by the time the constable turned into the yard, Margery had sternly dismissed the two maids who had been good for nothing all morning, in anticipation of the constable's visit.

'Put the mats on the line and give them a good beating,' she ordered, 'and don't come back until you're sent for. And as for you, Ned Makepeace, take Hugh and run away and play. There'll be things said here today as ain't fit for young ears.'

The boys left the room obediently enough, but as soon as they were out of earshot they scurried round the side of the house and crouched down under the open lattice, where they could hear every word that passed inside.

In the centre of it all sat Meg, in a place of honour in her father's chair. Her everyday brown dress had been brushed carefully, and Margery had supplied her with a clean white apron of her own. Her hair was pulled back and hidden by her white cap, a duplicate of the one worn by her sister-in-law. She waited demurely, with her hands folded in her lap. Only she knew how fast her heart was thumping in her breast.

'Now then, Meg,' Tom began, his tone hearty. 'Tell us about yesterday. What you saw, and what you did.'

She raised frightened eyes to his. 'I've already said. Over and over. Hasn't Dad told you?' Ben made an encouraging wave of his hand, as if to reassure her.

'Aye, he's told me, but I want to hear it from you. Ben wasn't there when it happened, and you were. Take it from the beginning, if you please.'

'Well, I wanted to visit Mumma's grave, so I went up to the churchyard.'

'And you met nobody on the road, not even a person passing by?'

'No. Nobody at all.'

'Go on, then.'

'I sat by the grave for a bit, and then I thought I'd go and have a look at the other graves. You know, where the old ones are buried, round the corner by the yews. And I never got that far because I came upon that . . . man, just lying there.' She fumbled in her pocket for her handkerchief, needing to mop her eyes before she went on.

'And you moved him, Meg. Why was that?'

'I wouldn't have touched him if I'd known he was a deader,' she shuddered, 'but I thought he must be ill and needing help. I rolled him over, and then I saw.'

She began to cry, great wrenching sobs that shook her slight body. Ben reached over and grasped her shoulder, murmuring soothing words.

Tom grimaced. 'All right, Meg; We'll say no more about that, but I do have more questions for you, if you're up to it.' She nodded.

'Now, then. This is very important. Think carefully before you answer me. When you were kneeling at your mother's grave, what did you hear?'

'Nothing, Tom. Nothing at all.'

'Try again. It's never completely quiet at that time of the morning.'

'There were birds, of course; twitting about all over the place, and I could hear the doves. Oh, and there was a dog barking, somewhere way off.'

'But nothing closer? The sound of a man working with a scythe, perhaps? People talking? Did you hear the church door opening, for instance?'

Meg shook her head. 'Nothing like that. Not a sound.'

'Did you see anything, then, apart from what you found? Somebody nipping over the style into Hundred Acre Field, for instance?'

Again she shook her head. Frustrated, Tom pulled a face at Adam, who shrugged.

'Is that all?' Meg asked, looking up into Tom's face. 'I'm sorry I couldn't help.'

'I don't have any more questions, at least, not at present. I do have one thing to say, though.' He looked at Ben for guidance. Seeing his dilemma, Ben took his daughter by the shoulders and came out with it.

'It's like this, gal. You said the body was warm to the touch when you rolled it over.'

'Yes, Dad?'

'Then that means he wasn't long dead. I think what Tom is trying to say is that whoever killed him wouldn't have had time to get far. He may have been lurking close by, crouched down behind one of them tall gravestones, mebbe.'

'But I've already told you I didn't see a thing!' Meg was indignant now. 'Why do you keep at me and at me?'

Tom's glance was steady. 'Ah, but the murderer can't know that, not for certain. You didn't see him, but mebbe he saw you. And I can guess what's going through his mind right now. Did she see me? Did she notice some little thing that will come back to her later on? You could be in danger, Meg. If he believes he has something to fear from you, he may try to silence you. You say that you ran out of the graveyard as soon as you realised what had happened; if it hadn't been for that you might not be sitting here now!'

'Oh!' Terrified, Meg began rocking back and forth in her chair. Margery, who had been quiet until now, spoke up briskly.

'Then Meg must stay indoors until this blows over. No murderer will get past me! He won't dare to try anything with all of us in the house, and I am sure the constable will have him behind bars in no time. Have you anyone in mind, Tom?'

'I do have one or two things up my

sleeve, mistress, but more than that I can't say at present.'

'I understand.' Margery made the offer of something to eat and drink, but he refused, saying he had to get on.

'And so must we, lad.' Ben nodded. 'Half the day gone, and not much work accomplished.'

'And you can send those lazy girls back while you're about it,' Margery directed, as the three men left the room. 'Goodness knows where they've got to; they could have beaten a dozen rugs by now! As for you, Meg Makepeace, work is what you need to take your mind off things. You can polish my good table, and put your elbow into it. And when you've done that you can pluck those chickens, and be careful about it. I'm saving the feathers for pillows, in case you've forgotten!'

It would take more than a little murder to stop Margery in her tracks, Meg reflected, but in this case the woman was probably right. Anything to erase the awful picture that came into her head every time she closed her eyes. Despite the chamomile drink Margery had brewed for her the previous evening she had slept badly, haunted by dreams of the dead man with the gaping wound at his throat.

Tom Woodcock mounted his horse and rode away. The first thing he had to do was to see the priest, Father Wagstaffe. In his own mind, old Josh was chief suspect, but it wouldn't do to go making accusations without first having something to go on. The priest hasn't been at home the day before, which Tom had known ahead of time because that was the first person Meg had run to after finding the corpse.

'I was out and about in the parish,' the old priest explained, when Tom eventually ran him to earth. 'People need to be kept up to the mark, and if they won't come to me, then I must go to them. You've come about this murder, of course. Any idea who the fellow is? We've got him lying in the church, but nobody seems to know his face, or what he was doing here.'

'So you didn't put him to work outside, then? He wasn't some out-of-work man, travelling the roads, who came to you, looking for alms?'

'Not that I know of, and if he had come to me I wouldn't have told him to work in the graveyard. That's old Josh's job and as far as I know his only income. I couldn't take that away from him. He's an idle fellow at times but which of us is perfect? If it comes to making a choice between providing work for one of my flock and a passing stranger, why, I have to look after our own. I might have provided the chap with a mug of ale and a crust before sending him on his way, but, as I said, I wasn't here when he called. If, that is, he came to my door at all,' the priest added, as an afterthought.

'That's that, then.' Tom sighed.

'So what do you mean to do now, then?'

'Ask all around, I suppose, see if

anyone remembers seeing a stranger round about.'

'Two strangers, don't you mean? This poor fellow, and the one who killed him?'

'We don't know that he was killed by a stranger, Father.'

The priest raised his bushy eyebrows at that. 'Surely not by one of our people here? Apart from anything else, why kill someone you've never met before? I could see it happening in the heat of the moment; say you caught him breaking into your house to steal your goods, or perhaps he laid hands on your wife or daughter, but neither was the case here. Unless you can find some similar motive, I'd say it's highly unlikely that the crime was committed by someone from this parish.'

Tom rode off, thinking furiously. At present, old Josh was his only suspect, and that only because a scythe was the murder weapon. But what could the motive have been? The man lived with his daughter and her unruly brood in a run-down cottage on the edge of the common, and he was sure they owned nothing worth stealing. And poor scraggy Jerusha was not the sort to attract the notice of a lustful stranger.

5

The joiner always kept one or two coffins on hand, in case they were needed in a hurry. It was an unfortunate fact that when somebody contracted an illness of some sort it tended to strike again in the same household. It was not unusual for several members of a family to die within a week. Thus it was possible for the murdered man to be fitted into one of the cheaper coffins within hours of his demise.

This had been placed on trestles in the church, with sand prudently spread on the floor beneath, to minimise the risk of damage to that holy place. Like Caesar Augustus of old, Tom Woodcock had decreed that everyone from the hamlet and the farmsteads on the outskirts should come together at an appointed time, not to be taxed, but to view the body. For, as he remarked to

Adam Makepeace, the longer the chap remained unidentified, the harder it would be to find his killer.

The people needed no persuasion to make them turn up. Nothing half as exciting had happened in Meppershall for many a long day and it was ghoulish curiosity that led most to gaze on the dead man's face. Not that there was anything much to be seen. The great gash in his throat was decently covered with a clean white cloth and the victim might well have been sleeping there, if not for the fact that his visage was pale in death.

One after another men, women, and children over the age of seven glanced at the corpse and shook their heads with regret.

'Shouldn't have put the coins on his eyelids yet,' one old gaffer grumbled.

'Why's that, then?' Tom enquired, knowing full well what was coming next.

'Why, everyone knows what happens if you gets yourself murdered. The killer's face gets shown in the deader's eyes. You could've saved yourself all this lining up to take a look at this 'un!'

'Believe me, I took a good look at his eyes before they laid him out, and there was nothing there, not even my own reflection.'

The priest had been standing watchfully by while all this had been going on. When it was over he remarked that the thing was settled; the corpse was obviously that of a stranger.

'Can you swear to that, Father?'

'Come now, Woodcock! Do you think I don't know my own parishioners? Nobody has gone missing. As to whether the man was dispatched by one of our own, every last one of them has turned up here today, showing no fear or anxiety. I feel sure that the murderer must also be a stranger.'

He thought for a moment and amended this. 'The widow Porter didn't come because she's been sick in her bed for some days past. That I can vouch for, having visited her only this morning. And, of course, old Josh has gone to ground somewhere, but you already knew that.'

It wasn't strictly true that everyone had taken part in the parade. The Makepeace household had been excused, on account of Meg having discovered the crime and Ben and Adam having been with Tom, looking for clues. Adam's suggestion that his wife stay out of it, on account of her whereabouts being known at the time the man was done to death, was met with indignation.

'I know my duty, husband!' she snapped. 'The whole hamlet has been summoned to appear, and go I shall!'

'I only thought . . . '

'I know what you thought, Adam Makepeace! I'm nought but a housewife. See nothing, hear nothing, just get on with your work! Well, I had a life before I married you, living miles from here, and it may be that I've seen this man in the past. I shall take a look at him with all the rest.'

Adam thought he knew what this was

all about, but wisely he held his tongue. Despite the fact that Margery had married into the well respected Makepeace family, the local women still held her in awe because she was an incomer. She wasn't one of them, having come from elsewhere in the shire, and it would take time for her to be accepted. Things would be different today. They would gather round her, all agog to hear what she had to say, for hadn't her own sister-in-law come across the body?

On the fringe of the little knot of listeners there was one person who stood slightly apart from the rest, listening with great attention. The questions that came from the crowd were just as important to that watcher as the response given by the blacksmith's wife. But, when all was said and done, she knew no more than the others, and possibly less than some.

'I'll see you home, Mistress Makepeace,' Tom said, appearing at Margery's elbow when the crowd had thinned out.

'I need to speak to Meg again.'

'Just so long as folk don't think I'm under arrest!' Margery sniffed, only half joking.

He laughed. 'No fear of that, mistress! No, I have to go to Bedford town to speak to the sheriff. I've heard he's there at present. I'll have to let him know what's happened here before I'm very much older.'

The sheriff held sway over both shires, Bedford and Northampton, and obviously he was unable to investigate every crime that happened within their borders, nor did he want to, for he was not a man to stir himself unduly. Still, it was wise to let him think he was in charge of all, in case something went wrong and he was casting about for someone to blame.

'Very wise,' Margery agreed, 'but what has this to do with Meg?'

'I was thinking she might come with me to Bedford.'

'Go with you all the way to Bedford! Whatever for?'

'It may be that the sheriff will want to speak to Meg himself, since she found the body. I'm just thinking ahead, that's all.'

'But she's already told her tale to you, and more than once! Does he not trust you then?'

'It's not a case of trust,' Tom answered, through gritted teeth. 'I'm in charge here and I'm sure I do my best. Trouble is, he's my superior, and if he takes it into his head to do something, who am I to stop him? I just think that if Meg comes with me she'll be there on the spot if he does wish to question her, and that will save him coming all the way down to Meppershall on purpose.' (And sticking his nose in where it's not wanted, he could have said, but such talk was unwise, especially when a woman such as Margery Makepeace was involved, sharp-tongued as she was.)

When they arrived at the house Tom found Meg quietly polishing a toasting fork. Several other items of houseware lay on the scrubbed table beside her. He was pleased to see that Ben was also present. If anyone could overrule Margery it was her father-in-law. He repeated what he'd already said to Adam's wife.

Meg bit her lip. 'I don't know what to say, Tom. It's a long way to go, especially there and back in one day. What if we were delayed, and couldn't set out again before dark?'

'No problem there!' he said heartily. 'My dad's old aunt keeps a lodging house in the town. She'd put us up if worse came to worst, and no one could make a better chaperone, if it's your reputation you're thinking of! What do you think, Ben?'

'I think it's a fine notion. It would do the girl good to have a change of scene, after what she's been through.' He opened the leather purse he wore at his belt, and brought out some coins. 'Here, gal! You have a look around the shops and see what you can find. Buy yourself some new headgear or summat!'

So it was settled. After agreeing to collect Meg the following morning at first light Tom went off, whistling. The idea that Meg might be needed to give evidence at Bedford was just an excuse. Tom knew Sheriff Bowman and it was highly unlikely that he'd worry his head too much over the death of one unknown dead man when Tom was on the spot to do the donkey work. That's what constables were for! So long as the crime was solved in short order, he'd be well satisfied.

No, what Tom Woodcock wanted was to get Meg all to himself for a time, so she could get to know him better. That is to say, he'd known her all her life, but there was always somebody else around, and he was sure she didn't think of him as sweetheart material. It was time he thought of getting wed. Meg was a pretty dear, and good natured with it. He could do worse.

Meg, of course, knew quite well what he was up to. As she might have said, if asked, 'I'm not as green as I'm cabbage looking.' When a man makes sheep's eyes at a maid, something is afoot! She was surprised that Margery hadn't noticed, and said something.

The question was, did Meg want Tom Woodcock for a sweetheart? He'd been a boyhood friend of her older brothers, Adam and Harry — he still was Adam's friend, for that matter — and she still remembered their rough teasing. How she'd resented being told to run away and play, when she'd attempted to join in their activities!

She smiled to herself. She'd allowed herself to fantasise about Tom's motives now. All he'd done was to invite her to go along with him in the morning. That was hardly a proposal of marriage! And if Tom did try to pressure her into a relationship she didn't want, she could always say she'd believed his tale about going to see the sheriff. That way, she couldn't be accused of playing fast and loose with his affections.

Dad was right; the outing would do her a power of good. She'd go along and enjoy herself.

'Who's going to pay for all this? That's what I'd like to know!'

The speaker stared gloomily into the hole which would eventually become the last resting place of the stranger. The digger straightened up, wiping the sweat from his face, leaving a muddy trail behind.

'How would I know? Priest says dig his grave, so I digs.'

'Ah, but will you get paid for it, I wonder? It's not just the grave, is it? There's the coffin as well. Costs money, that do, and Martin Cole don't give them away. And what about Father Wagstaffe? Don't he get paid for saying the words over the corpse? And I don't suppose they'll toll the passing bell. How could they? Nobody knows how old he was so how many strokes would they give, you tell me that!'

'Unless you mean to come down here and give me a hand, Amos Denton, you get off and let me get on with my work, else I'll be here all day.'

'All right, all right, keep your hair on! I was only saying what everybody else is thinking! No harm in that, is there?' The man wandered off, whistling. He could just make out a figure in the distance, staggering along the road as though buffeted by a strong wind.

'Josh Palmer, by all that's holy.' He quickened his steps. Here was his chance to get in on something interesting.

'Where've you been all this time, Josh?'

'Who wants to know?' the voice was slurred.

'You know me, Josh. Amos Denton.'

'Oh, yesh?'

'I said, where have you been? Constable's been looking for you.'

'None of your business, nor his, neither.' Josh continued on his way, muttering.

'He's been on a bender,' Amos mused, stating the obvious. 'The question is, why now?' Periodically Josh did disappear for a few days, having imbibed too freely, but it was usually after something had happened that he'd rather forget, and, if you'd killed a man, wouldn't that be an excuse for seeking oblivion? More fool him to come back to Meppershall if that were the case.

Always happy to be the bearer of news, good or bad, Amos turned towards Tom Woodcock's cottage. The sooner the constable had old Josh in custody, the better. When he arrived he found the door firmly locked. He thumped and rattled to no avail, rousing a neighbour in the process.

'If you're looking for Tom, he ain't there,' the woman shrilled. 'And I'll thank you to stop making that noise. I've been up half the night with our John teething, and I was just catching forty winks before the child starts up again.'

'Sorry, missus! It's just that old Josh is back, and the constable needs to know.'

'Well, it's no good telling me, is it?' She shut the window with a bang. The wails of a child in misery filled the air.

Amos wandered off, disconsolate. Time hung heavily on his hands since he'd stopped work as the village cobbler. He'd been willing to carry on but nature had defeated him. He was getting on in years now and his hands had become too shaky to allow him to work. Luckily he had enough put by to keep him in reasonable comfort, but he missed having a purpose in life. He was secretly disgusted with himself for having descended to the level of the village gossip.

He heard the sound of a horse approaching, clip clopping along at a steady pace. It was a rather nice chestnut gelding, ridden by a man whom Amos had never seen before. His eyes brightened. He waited until the man drew near before calling out to him.

'Can I help you, master? You'll be needing directions, mebbe?'

'No, thanks. I'm bound for the church; I know my way.' The horse strode on.

Amos had no wish to go home, where he'd only spend the rest of the day staring at the four walls. He wanted someone to talk to. He'd go to the forge, he thought. There was bound to be somebody there; there always was.

'Good day to you, Amos,' Ben smiled. 'Lost your way, have you?'

'I was seeking Tom Woodcock, as it happens.'

'Well, man, you won't find him here, less he's hiding under that bench there!'

'I know that, Ben! Not stupid, am I? He's nowhere to be found, and I thought you might know where he is.'

'Gone to Bedford,' Adam put in. 'Gone to see the sheriff, he says, asking what he's supposed to do about this murder.'

'Ah! Now that's where I can help him. Old Josh is back, drunk as a coot. Won't say where he's been, or why, but I daresay Woodcock can wring it out of him.'

'If Tom passes here on his way back, we'll let him know, Amos.'

59

'Ah, but that's not all, see. A stranger on a horse passed me on the road here, not ten minutes back. Spoke to him, I did.'

'Oh, yes?' Ben gave him a look that spoke of his exasperation. He felt like saying that they had work to do, and he wished that the old man would go on his way and let them get on with it. Amos interpreted this look correctly and was rightfully annoyed. He spoke slowly, grinding out every word so there was no mistaking the message he meant to convey.

'He was going to the church. He said he knew the way. Now, what does that tell you? One stranger gets himself done in and they find his corpse up at the church yard. Now another stranger comes along, going to the same place, or pretty near!'

'And you're afraid the grim reaper might get him as well, then?'

'No need for you to scoff, Ben Makepeace! How come this chap knows the way to our church unless he's been here before?'

'Apart from the fact you can see the steeple for miles around, you mean?'

Amos ignored this. 'I say he's the murderer, returning to the scene of the crime. He wants to see what's been happening since he did the deed.'

'More fool him, then,' Adam sniffed, bending over the anvil. Finding nothing more to say, Amos shuffled off.

'Silly old fool,' Ben muttered. 'Still, it wouldn't hurt for Tom to look into it, I suppose. You'd think we'd never had wayfarers passing through the hamlet before. Now everyone's a potential thief and murderer.'

'Folks are jittery, Dad, that's the trouble. Who do you think did it? Old Josh?'

'Could be, boy, but where's the motive? And say he did it in self defence, why should this foreigner have attacked him? It's not as if Josh had anything worth stealing. And why would anyone have had a grudge against him, bad enough to come and attack him for? We know he's a drunken fool, but he's harmless with it. If there was any vice in him I doubt the priest would let him work on church lands.'

'And, as we already know, robbery wasn't the motive for the killing.'

Like all the neighbours, they were simply going round in circles. Unless the dead man could be identified, it seemed unlikely that the crime would ever be solved. The murder would become a nine days' wonder, and after that something new would capture their attention.

The story would become part of local folklore, to be brought out and inspected around the hearth fires on winter evenings, and laid to rest again.

Up at the church, Father Wagstaffe was exclaiming with pleasure over the fine new bridle which had just been handed over to him.

'Good workmanship, John, good workmanship! This should see me out, no mistake about that. I must say I didn't expect to get it so soon, but I'm glad to have it. My old one was past mending, and it doesn't look well for the priest's horse to be going about with its bridle knotted with bits of old rope.'

John Dilley grinned. 'I don't know so much! You priests always seem to have your hands out for money. The poorer you look, the more people are likely to give. Now you have this fine bridle they'll say you must be well off to be able to afford it. P'raps I should take it home again. What do you say, Father?'

'None of your cheek, my son!' The priest's lips curved in an answering smile. 'I take it you won't say no to a tankard of ale before you start on the return journey? Let your horse into the graveyard, then, and we'll go inside. He can cut the grass for me. I've been thinking of turning my own Brownie out there for a while. The man who usually looks after things hasn't been seen for a few days. He's been on a bender, no doubt. It certainly wouldn't be the first time. I suppose you've heard about the murder we've had here?'

'I did hear something, but I didn't get the details.'

'A stranger had his throat cut, just around the corner there. The blacksmith's daughter found him lying in the grass, poor girl.'

'And nobody knows who he was?'

'Indeed not. Unfortunately he's just been buried, or I'd ask you to take a look at him. See if you happen to recognise him. Come on inside, my son, and we'll have that drink. It's thirsty work, standing here gossiping!'

John Dilley needed no further invitation. He followed the priest into the house.

6

'How will you know where to find the sheriff?' Meg wondered. She hoped they'd be able to stop soon. She was riding pillion and it seemed as if they'd been on the road forever. She was beginning to feel sore in an unmentionable spot.

'We'll try the gaol first; that's the most likely place. I heard he was in Bedford on another case, so he won't be far away from the centre of things. If he's not there, we'll have to do the rounds of the taverns. He'll be in one of them, I have no doubt.'

'Is the man such a drunkard, then?' Meg wondered.

'Hush, now! We don't want to be overheard saying things like that!'

She looked around. 'Where's the harm? There's not a soul in sight.'

'It's always wise to guard one's

tongue,' he said mysteriously. 'I don't know what Bowman's habits are, but taverns aren't just for drinking in, you know; not when you're on the side of the law. You go there to listen to gossip, see? You might hear something useful.'

'Gossip!' Meg was scornful. 'I know what that means. A lot of silly talk, most of it made up, and some poor soul on the receiving end gets punished for no good reason.'

'This is different, Meg. I'm not talking about a lot of spiteful old women standing around the village pump when they should be at home, attending to their duties!'

She shrugged. She didn't care where they went next, just so long as she could get down off this great horse and stretch her legs.

Luckily the sheriff was at the gaol when they arrived. The turnkey looked Tom up and down and told him to tether the horse, while he went to inquire if Master Bowman would see him.

'He'll see me, all right.' Tom was firm. 'I've come to report a murder, and if you try to turn me away you'll be in trouble, my good man!'

Grumbling, the man ambled inside, returning shortly to say that Tom might go in.

'Don't wander far, Meg; I'll call you if you're needed.'

'I want a look at the shops,' she pouted.

'We can do that later. Just do as I say for now. Remember why we're here.'

Robert Bowman was a big, burly man, who would have made two of Tom. *Pity the Villain who tries to get the best of him!* Tom thought. *Even the grim reaper would have difficulty subduing this one!*

But the sheriff seemed a decent enough sort. He listened intently to Tom's story before asking what the chances were of catching the killer.

'There's not much to go on at the moment,' Tom admitted. 'I've brought Meg Makepeace with me today; she's the young woman who found the corpse. She's willing to talk to you if you want.'

'Did she see or hear anything that might help your enquiries?'

Tom shook his head. 'That's the strange part. According to her, everything was quiet as the grave.' He winced, recognising his unfortunate choice of words. Bowman appeared not to notice.

'I shan't bother, then. I suppose you're satisfied with her tale? She's a truthful sort of maid? Then I'll leave you to get on with it, Woodcock. I can't spare the time to come down to Meppershall. I've a very nasty investigation at the moment. Somebody has been stalking young women and then attacking them in their homes when they're on their own.'

'We have a fellow in custody but so far we can't prove anything. He's protesting his innocence, loud and clear, but then he would, wouldn't he? He doesn't want to swing, which he will do, if I can find the smallest piece of evidence against him.'

'Then I won't hold you up any longer, sir,' Tom told him.

Untying his horse, he went to find Meg, who was strolling across a piece of open ground, towards the Ouse. She looked so relieved when he announced that the sheriff didn't want to see her that he almost regretted having brought her along under false pretences, simply for the pleasure of her company.

'Are we travelling home tonight?' she asked, when they had eaten and then spent a pleasurable hour going in and out of the shops.

'Do you want to?' he asked, hoping that the answer would be no.

'I'd just as soon have a good night's rest, and start back fresh first thing in the morning,' she pleaded. 'That's if you meant what you said about your aunt letting lodgings?'

'I did indeed, and we'll go there right away, to see if she has room to spare. For if she does not, then we shall indeed have to start for home before the daylight fades.'

Mistress Wilmot greeted them with delight. 'I'm sure we can squeeze you in somewhere, Thomas! And you, my gal, if you don't mind sharing with my two serving wenches, you can have the garret at no charge!'

When Meg had been dispatched upstairs with a jug of water and clean towel, Anne Wilmot grinned shyly at her nephew's son.

'And very nice, too! She's the one you intend to marry, I take it?'

'If she'll have me, yes; but it's early days, Aunt, so don't go spoiling things by talking out of turn.'

'You mean she ain't got wind of your intentions yet!'

'That's about it.'

'Then don't you worry. I shan't say a word. Known her long, have you?'

'All her life, Aunt. I grew up alongside her brothers, Adam and Harry Makepeace. Adam and his dad are the blacksmiths at Meppershall.'

'A good trade,' she mused. 'Will she want to tie herself down to a village constable, I wonder, who spends all his days sorting out wrong doers? She might think it a bit of a come-down.'

'Mine is an honest trade, Aunt, and in any case I believe she might be glad to get out of her father's house. Adam has married again, and his new wife stands very much on her rights, putting Meg's nose out of joint. Ever since her mother died, and then his poor Bess, Meg has ruled the roost, and now she must stand aside to make way for the newcomer.'

'Not a happy situation, I agree, but it would be unwise to rush into marriage on that account. Unless the girl loves you, it could be a case of out of the frying pan, into the fire, for you as well as her. Would you wish to be trapped in a loveless marriage for the rest of your life?'

'We shall see,' Tom replied. He had heard a light step on the stair and the last thing he wanted was for Meg to guess at his feelings prematurely. He quickly changed the subject.

'What news of the wider world, Aunt? I hear you've had a murder in these parts, too.'

'More than one, lad.' She nodded pleasantly at Meg, who was looking much refreshed after her wash. 'Still, they've caught the fellow now and he'll swing before long, and that will be that.'

'They've got to find him guilty yet,' Tom reminded her.

'Pshaw! Of course he's guilty. He was all set to do away with another poor woman when her husband came on the scene and caught him crouching down behind their garden wall, just waiting his chance to spring! If that's not guilty, I don't know what is!'

Meg gulped and sat down suddenly. Anne Wilmot grimaced. 'That's enough of that kind of talk, I think! Let me tell you what I heard yesterday! Two men stopped here overnight, they left just before you two arrived, and such a tale they had to tell of the goings on at

Court! They do say that the king is bound and determined to put his wife aside. This latest light of love of his, Nan Bullen as they call her, is insisting on marriage, if you please, before she grants him her favours.'

'Of course, the man is besotted and can't see that it's not him she's after, but that she longs to be Queen of England! If she gets her way, poor dear Catherine will be out in the cold, and her such a good and faithful wife, by all accounts.'

'But he can't do that, can he?' Meg was horrified.

'My dear, kings can do whatever they please. If he wants the chit, he'll find a way.'

'I don't see how. Till death us do part. Isn't that what couples vow when they wed?'

Mistress Wilmot glanced over her shoulder. 'And that can be arranged, I'm sure,' she whispered. 'It wouldn't be the first time that some king or queen was got out of the way by means of poison or the like. Poor Catherine will be said to die from some disease and then, after a decent interval, old Harry, the grieving widower, will wed again. Nobody will believe a word of it, of course, but who would dare to voice such an opinion? He'd be found floating in the Thames with his throat cut, before he was very much older.'

Tom sighed. He loved his aunt, but she was too outspoken by half. In one breath she'd spoken treason and at the same time managed to remind Meg once again of what she'd sooner forget!

'The king has had mistresses before,' he reminded her. 'Mary Boleyn, this Anne's sister, among them. Then there was Bessie Blount, who has a son by him. He dallied with them all for a time and then moved on to greener pastures, as they say. He'll tire of this Nan in time, especially if she keeps him hankering for what he wants. Just you wait and see.'

'Mebbe, mebbe not,' his aunt sniffed. She wasn't about to give up her interest in the king's affairs, and neither was any other right-minded woman in England!

★ ★ ★

'What a shame you had to go traipsing all the way to Bedford for nothing,' Ben Makepeace remarked, tongue in cheek. He had a pretty shrewd idea as to why the constable had wanted Meg to make the journey with him. While he didn't want to lose his only daughter any time soon, she had to wed some day, and she could go farther and fare worse than to choose Tom Woodcock.

The tips of Tom's ears turned pink, although this may have been a result of the heat in the forge, where they were standing. 'It won't hurt none if the sheriff thinks I'm keen to get on with the job. For all I knew the man would have come down to Meppershall, if I hadn't gone to him first, and that I don't want.'

'You'd have been better off staying here,' Adam remarked. 'Old Josh almer has come wandering back, and you'd best have a word with him before he goes to ground again.'

'No need telling me how to do my job, Adam Makepeace! Do I come telling you how to fashion a shoe?'

Adam grinned. They'd been friends ever since they'd been out of swaddling clothes, and over the years many a friendly insult had passed between them.

'Better yet, there's a stranger been seen hanging around the church. Amos Denton reported that. It seems he went to your place but you were nowhere to be found. Gone gallivanting to Bedford, we told him.'

'That's more like it. I'd best get up there to see what I can see.'

'Not much point, I'd say. He'll be far away by now. Might as well go home and put your feet up, Tom, instead of standing about here, keeping honest men from their daily toil.'

Tom made a rude noise and sauntered off.

Palmer's cottage, about a mile outside the hamlet, was a run down daub and wattle affair, with the pathway to the entrance obscured by nettles. For a man who was so handy wielding a scythe, one would have expected his garden to have been in better condition, Tom reflected. Seemingly Palmer was the type of man who did the minimum possible amount of labour to earn himself a wage, and left it at that.

The door was flung open by a slatternly woman with several small children clinging to her skirts. He assumed she was Palmer's daughter, although since the family were relative newcomers to Meppershall, he could not be sure. However, she knew who he was.

'You come looking for Dad, I s'pose,' she muttered. 'Leave off doing that, young Will; haven't I told yer?' This was directed to a ragged boy who was busily wiping his nose on his sleeve.

'There was nobody home when I

came before, Mistress . . . ?'

'Oakley. I was married once upon a time to Will Oakley, over to Southill, though much good it did me!'

'Your husband is dead, then?'

The woman shrugged. 'Could be, for all I know or care. He gave me this lot, and then run off. Nothing for it but I had to come here to Dad. It's not exactly Windsor Castle, but it's a roof over our heads.'

'I need to talk to Josh,' Tom told her. 'Is he in?'

'Not him. Could be anywhere, this time of day. Come back about dinner time, constable. P'raps he'll be here then.'

Tom nodded. 'I don't suppose you've seen a stranger hereabouts, have you? I heard tell there was a man in the neighbourhood yesterday.'

She shook her head. 'No strangers, Master. Never a one. O' course, I been busy in the house so I wouldn't know what's going on in the world, would I?'

He got away before she could inflict

any more of her bitter ramblings on him. As he so often did, he gave thanks for having been born male. As far as he was concerned, being a woman had little to recommend it.

He now turned his steps towards the church. For a wonder, the old priest was at home. Tom found him in the little field behind the house, poking around among the bee hives.

'Have you caught our murderer yet?' he shouted, by way of greeting.

'Hot on the trail,' Tom countered, as he came closer. In truth he was no farther ahead than he had been on the day the corpse was discovered, but he had his reputation to think of and could not let that be known, even to the priest. It was important that people should think he had some skill that made him better suited to the art of detection than the common man. 'I heard you had a stranger here yesterday. Is that so?'

'Now that depends on what you mean by a stranger,' Father Wagstaffe replied. 'If you mean somebody not known to me, no, I didn't. If you mean someone from outside the village, yes. John Dilley called on me yesterday.'

'Isn't he the harness maker from Southill? What was he doing here?'

'Not that it's any of your business, my son, but he was here delivering a fine new bridle I'd ordered. The chin strap was broken on the old one and it was worn so thin in other places I was afraid something would snap one of these days, when I was least expecting it. Old Brownie is quiet enough as a general rule, but if something spooks him he's inclined to bolt, and I've no wish to find myself lying on the ground with a broken leg, or worse.'

'I suppose I'll have to go over to Southill and speak to him, then.'

'No need for that, my son. I've given him my old satchel to mend, where the stitching was coming apart. When he brings it back I'll send him to you. How will that be?'

Tom frowned. 'Why didn't you give

him the satchel the first time he was here, Father? It would have saved him a trip.'

'Because I sent him my order by way of the carter, Tom. John never was here before yesterday.'

'As far as we know,' Tom muttered. Sensing that the old priest was anxious to get on with his work, he bade him goodbye and set off home. On the way he met Amos Denton who was wandering along the lane, taking swipes at the vegetation with his walking stick.

'Hey, Amos!' he shouted, breaking into a trot. 'I want a word with you!'

'And I've already tried to have a word with you!' the old man sniffed. 'Only you'd vanished off the face of the earth. Supposed to be the constable, you are, but never around when you're wanted. What good's that, eh?'

Tom ignored the slur. 'I'm told you met a stranger here yesterday.'

'What of it?' Plainly Amos was not about to give in without a fight.

'Just describe him, will you?'

The old man shrugged. 'Not much to tell. Ordinary sort of chap; brown hair, regular clothes, all dusty from the road. Nice horse, though. A chestnut gelding, stepping out proud, like.'

'How tall, would you?'

'About sixteen hands, I reckon.'

'The man, you fool, not the horse!'

'How do I know? He never got down from his horse. Like I said, just ordinary.'

'Tell me what he said, Amos.' Tom had already heard this from Adam Makepeace, but he wanted to get it from the horse's mouth.

'Not much of anything. It was me spoke to him first, see. Seeing he was a stranger, like, I asked him if he needed directions, but he just shook his head. Said he was going to the church and he knew his way.'

'Are you sure that's what he said? That bit about knowing the way?'

'Course I'm sure. Not simple, am I?'

Tom thanked the old man and continued on. Something wasn't right here. Hadn't the priest said he'd sent his order to Dilley by way of the carter? So the first time the harness maker had cause to come to the church it was the day he made the delivery. Had he lied to old Amos?

Not that this meant anything. Southill wasn't that far away. The man could have come here in the past for any number of reasons, even attended a wedding or funeral Mass at the church.

Say that was true, Tom reasoned. Why would he have done that? Might it be that he was related to people in Meppershall? Or related to someone who had married into a local family? That would have to be looked into. On the other hand, what would that have to do with anything? It was not a Meppershall man who had been murdered.

At the moment, the only thread connecting Dilley and the murdered man was that both were strangers to the hamlet, and that meant nothing at all. Tom reached down and snapped off a blade of grass which he proceeded to chew on.

Looking at it from another direction, say that Dilley did have some grudge against the murdered man. Or perhaps Dilley had committed some crime, and the other man had witnessed it, and had to be silenced. All possible. But then why do the deed in Meppershall, of all places? None of it made any sense.

7

Meg was drawn back to the scene of the crime. Today would have been her niece's birthday, and she wanted to take flowers to place on the grave. At least, that was her excuse. She still dreamed about the corpse she'd found lying in the grass, and she reasoned that if she visited the spot and found it peaceful the awful images would be exorcised.

Having deposited her flowers and murmured a brief prayer for the repose of the child's soul, she rounded the corner, her heart thumping. There was nothing to be seen but the quiet graves. She realised she'd been holding her breath, and she let it go in a long sigh. The grass was taller now. Old Josh had not returned to tackle it. Perhaps he harboured a superstitious dread of handling the scythe which had been a murder weapon.

Some distance away, on the other side of the yews, there was a ridge where there were known to be unmarked graves. People had been buried there since time out of mind; plague victims, some of them, or folk who had no family plot. It was here that the murdered stranger had been laid to rest. Meg spotted a female figure approaching the site, all muffled in a shawl. She tiptoed into the shelter of the tallest yew, and waited.

The woman paused for a moment, looking over her shoulder before sinking down on her knees beside the murdered man's grave. Even at this distance it was easily recognisable because it was still bare; no vegetation had encroached upon it as yet.

Who was this woman, and why say prayers for a stranger? And if she was not imploring the saints to intercede for him, why was she kneeling? It was a mystery which needed to be solved. Meg shuffled closer.

The shawl fell back, revealing a head covered with iron grey hair. Meg recognised that head. She stepped forward.

'Good morrow, Mistress Sykes!'

The woman looked up, a momentary flash of alarm in her eyes. 'Meg Makepeace! You startled me. I fancied myself alone.'

'Did you know the dead man, Mistress?'

'Why, surely, you knew him better than I, for wasn't it you who discovered him as he lay dying?'

Meg was puzzled. 'I found the corpse, yes, but he was dead before I came there.'

'And you saw nothing, heard nothing?'

'Nothing at all, as I told Tom Woodcock. But if you did not know the man, why do you visit his grave?'

'I was passing by, and thought to say an Ave or two. It is a work of charity to pray for the dead, and this poor soul has no-one else to help him out of purgatory. You may take my place now, if you will.'

She struggled to her feet, waving off Meg's outstretched hand. Meg stared after the woman as she limped away. It was then that a horseman crossed her line of vision. A youngish man, sitting tall in the saddle, mounted on a chestnut gelding, riding up to the church. Picking up her skirts, Meg ran across the grass, reaching his side just as he dismounted. This must be the stranger she'd heard about from Adam and her father.

'Do I know you, mistress?' the fellow had a smile which lit up his whole face. She realised that her sudden appearance must seem odd to him. Not wanting to arouse his suspicions, she blurted out the first thing which came to mind.

'I wanted to see your horse,' she dimpled. A remark which would have been better suited to a ten-year-old child than a demure young woman!

'You like horses, then? Have you one of your own?'

'No, but the Makepeaces, my father

and brother, are blacksmiths and farriers here. They shoe all the horses hereabouts and treat them for ailments as well.'

'So they have taught you to be a good judge of horseflesh, then.'

But am I a good judge of men? Meg wondered, for she found herself liking this man, as though she had known and trusted him all her life. The point was, could he be trusted, or was he a wolf in sheep's clothing?

Father Wagstaffe came out of his house then, and the man slid from his horse and turned to address the priest. 'I've put a stitch or two in your satchel, Father, and it's good for a few years yet.'

'It should see me out, then! I see you've met young Meg Makepeace!'

'Mistress Meg came to admire my horse,' the fellow said, with a twinkle in his eye. The priest sent an old fashioned look her way. Meg blushed. She feared that both men believed her to be a shameless hussy, willing to accost any passing stranger, which was far from the truth. Still, she could hardly explain what was really on her mind. Fortunately the priest saved her the trouble of trying to worm secrets out of the man by directing him to call on the constable.

'Woodcock is investigating the murder we had here a few days past. No suspicion is attached to you, John Dilley, but he must talk to everyone.'

'I'll go gladly, though I was nowhere near Meppershall when the crime was committed. There is nothing I can tell him that will be of use, but there, I suppose he can rule me out when I've explained all.' Pocketing the coins the priest handed him, he looked up the lane, as if he expected Tom Woodcock to appear at any minute.

'Where can he be found, then, this constable?'

'At home at this time of day, I shouldn't wonder! I daresay Meg will be pleased enough to show you the way.'

'Then we'll walk together.' Dilley smiled. 'For never let it be said that I rode while a lovely young woman walked behind me!'

Tom Woodcock was at home when they arrived at his cottage. He came to the door, wiping his hands on his jerkin, leaving a damp patch on the cloth. His eyebrows raised, he looked from one to the other of them, awaiting an explanation. Both spoke at once.

'This is John Dilley . . . '

'I'm Dilley, the harness maker of Southill. The priest tells me you want to speak to me?'

'Yes, indeed. Come inside, if you don't mind the clutter. I was just tackling the washing up. There are times when a wife would come in handy!'

He stood aside to let Dilley enter. 'Thanks for bringing him, Meg. I shan't keep you any longer.'

With the door shut in her face, Meg stood still for a moment, fuming and embarrassed. What on earth was the matter with Tom, treating her like the village busybody, to be sent on her way? She wanted to know what Dilley was about to say. She pressed her ear to the door, but it was made of solid oak and any sound was effectively muzzled. Defeated, she turned her face towards home.

Meanwhile, Dilley had seated himself on a three-legged stool and was placidly answering questions. No, he was not in the habit of coming to Meppershall. Most of his trade took place between his workshop in Southill and Ampthill, except for taking a stall at a fair once in a while. He had only come here to the hamlet because the priest had sent for him.

Did he have kinfolk here? No. Had he ever been to the church before that first visit to the priest? No, he hadn't.

'Then how is it,' asked Tom, swooping in for the kill, 'that you told Amos Denton when he sought to direct you, that you knew the way to the church?'

Dilley looked puzzled. 'I don't think I . . .'

'An old gaffer. Stopped you in the lane, or so he says.'

'Ah! I remember now. No mystery about that, constable! Only one church in Meppershall, the carter told me, save for some old chapel and you can sight that from way off, it being the tallest building in the place!'

Deflated, Tom tried to think of other questions, the answers to which could lead to a connection between Dilley and the victim, but could not. 'Then you are free to go — for now.' He sniffed.

Dilley, however, was not done with him. 'That young woman, Meg Make-peace, I think she calls herself.'

'What about her?'

'Is she spoken for, do you know?'

'She's not betrothed, if that's what you mean!' Tom's expression had hardened. 'I'd advise you not to get any ideas about dalliance with her, though! She's a brother and a father to look after her, both brawny men. I pity the man who gets on the wrong side of that pair!'

'No need to get on your high horse, man! I was only asking!'

Dilley sauntered outside to where his horse was waiting and vaulted into the saddle.

Tom slammed the door behind the fellow, all his pleasure in the bright day evaporated after this encounter. He decided to have a word with Adam when he saw him next. This Dilley obviously had designs on Meg, and by the way she'd looked at him, the feeling was mutual.

He wanted Meg for himself but if he warned her against Dilley that might drive her right into the harness maker's arms. He must proceed with caution; women were like half-green horses; they needed careful handling.

A cart pulled by a limping horse rattled into the Makepeace yard. At the sound of their approach Adam straightened his back and looked out, seeing a tired looking man and a woman of around middle age. The man descended from the cart, passing the reigns into the hands of his female companion, although judging by the way the horse stood with its head drooping, there was little need to control the beast.

'Your horse has cast a shoe, I see,' Adam remarked. 'Gone lame, too, by the looks of it.' He went forward and ran a practiced hand over the animal's offside foreleg. 'Have you come far?'

'From just outside Windsor, Master Smith. We've been on the road for days, having taken a wrong turn in the mist one evening. Everyone we meet gives us wrong directions. If I'd known where we were at times I'd have been inclined to turn back!'

'That would not do at all!' his wife said firmly. 'We're bound for Bedford town, and get there we must. Our married daughter is about to have her first child, you see, and naturally she's sent for her mother! I suppose they have midwives in the town, but at times like this there's nobody like your own flesh and blood, is there?'

Adam and his father exchanged glances. Ben nodded. 'You're still off the main road to Bedford, friends. You'll not get there tonight, and besides, that mare of yours needs a rest. Take her out of the shafts and put her in the paddock there. My son will shoe her later. As for the pair of you, you'll stay here with us, and get an early start in the morning.'

The man started to protest but his wife clambered out of the cart, one hand clamped on her back. ''Tis very good of you, sir, and of course we shall pay for our night's lodging, just as we should have done at some hostelry along the way.'

Leaving Ben to deal with this, Adam went in search of his wife.

'We've guests, my dear,' he explained. 'They've lost their way and their horse has gone lame. Dad's invited them to stay the night.'

His wife hesitated. 'Strangers, husband? Is it safe, or should we be murdered in our beds this night?'

'Hardly likely. An older couple, the wife wanting to attend her daughter in childbed. Besides,' he added, in the manner of offering a carrot to a donkey, 'they've come all the way from Windsor, or near enough as makes no difference. No doubt they'll have interesting tales to tell of the goings on at Court.'

The castle employed hordes of ordinary people — cooks, laundresses and scullions — who always seemed to know what was going on in the ranks of their betters. Juicy gossip flowed fast and spread around the surrounding countryside like floods in spring.

Margery brightened. Aside from the murder of a man that nobody seemed to know, nothing of interest had happened of late. She relished the idea of being the first to hear news from Windsor, and of regaling her acquaintances with it.

'By all means bid them welcome,' she agreed. ''Tis only Christian to help poor souls in need.'

Adam hid a smile. He knew his Margery. Still, he had to admit that it would be good to hear news of the outside world. Meg had returned from Bedford with some story of high jinks at Court, gleaned from Tom Woodcock's great aunt. The king had a new mistress, Anne Boleyn, or, as the common people called her, Nan Bullen. Her sister, Mary Boleyn, had been his light o' love for some time, but the king had tired of her and taken up with her sister instead.

Their visitors were called Paston. The husband, Ambrose, a glover by trade, was a tall, wiry man, with a receding hairline. His wife, whose first name they never heard, was exceedingly anxious about their daughter, Barbara, who was married to a merchant of Bedford.

'For although I've borne nine, she's the only one to survive,' Mistress Paston explained, a tear in her eye. 'How I shall bear it if anything should happen to her now, I do not know. That's why I must be at her side when her travail comes upon her. At least I'll be there to bid her farewell if aught goes wrong!'

Meg's lip trembled and even Margery looked bleak. Adam decided it was time to change the subject.

'We've heard that the king has a new mistress,' he began.

Mistress Paston's eyes widened. 'Gracious me, you are behind the times. King Harry has been in love with that Bullen girl this long time, although whether she is in truth his mistress is another matter altogether! They do say as she refuses to grant him her favours, unless he makes her his wife!'

'Which can't happen unless something happens to the queen!' Margery was disappointed. She had hoped for something more exciting than the old, old story of a man, tired of an ageing wife, who had turned to a younger woman.

'But haven't you heard?' Mistress Paston sensed that her audience was losing interest. 'The king wants a divorce. They say he's appealed to the Pope himself. People say that he wants to marry again because his wife can't give him sons, and there must be male heirs to follow him.'

'But the queen has borne boys, hasn't she?' Margery puzzled.

'To be sure, but all of them died. Now the king believes that God won't give him living sons, all on account of him having married his brother's widow.'

'Rubbish!'

'Rubbish or not,' the older woman said, 'but by all accounts that's what he seems to believe. It's common knowledge! People are talking about it openly in the streets.'

'I daresay it'll all blow over,' Ben said calmly. 'One of these days the king will see another pretty face and he'll forget about this Nan, same as he did with her sister.'

'Ah, but there's more to it than that!' Paston remarked. 'I seen it with my own eyes, didn't I?'

'What's that?'

'Why, the queen's been sent to Rickmansworth, along with her whole household.'

'Where's Rickmansworth?' Meg wanted to know.

'It's in Hertfordshire, mistress. The queen's been sent to The More, which was one of Cardinal Wolsey's residences. The king wants her out of the way. I never saw such a procession in all my life. People on horses, baggage in wagons, even folk trudging along behind. I had to stand aside and wait for them to pass, and that made me late going to market.'

'And he had to bring my best butter home again because it didn't sell,' Mistress Paston mourned. 'You have to make an early start to get the best prices, and by the time my man got there it was too late. People had done their shopping and gone home, isn't that so, husband?'

'Mind you,' he mused, 'I wouldn't have missed it for the world. All those men and women in their fancy raiment, the like of which you never saw.'

'Did you see the queen?' Meg breathed.

'Well, no; but I saw the coach she was riding in.'

'How d'you know it was her, then?' Margery wasn't convinced.

'Had to be her, didn't it? All along the way people was cheering, shouting 'long live Queen Catherine' and 'down with Nan Bullen!' I wouldn't like to be in that Bullen woman's shoes if the crowd caught up with her! Pelted with rotten vegetables she'd be, and no mistake!'

'Poor lady!' Meg said. Royal the queen might be, a Spanish princess by birth and aunt to the Holy Roman Emperor, but it seemed she had her troubles like any other woman. 'What's to become of her now?'

'By what we've heard the king is still trying to get her to go quietly,' Mistress Paston sniffed, her expression grim. 'Agree that her marriage is no true union, and retire to a convent. Very religious she is, they say, always going to chapel and telling her beads, so she might as well retreat from the world. Trouble is, she won't admit to it. She keeps saying she's been a true and faithful wife and has never lived in sin!'

'I should think not, indeed!' Margery cried. 'After she's carried and given birth to all those children! It's not her fault if God seems fit to take them unto himself.'

'So if I set my heart on a younger woman and try to ship you to a nunnery, you won't go?' Adam grinned. His wife slapped him with the towel she was holding, and the serious mood dissipated.

When their visitors had gone on their way, the Makepeace household settled back into its ordinary routine, Meg's mind went back to the murdered man. Already her discovery of the corpse was beginning to seem like a nasty dream.

Meg remembered with a start that she hadn't said anything to Tom

Woodcock about the woman at the graveside. He'd shut the door in her face before she'd had the chance. Well, let him wait, then. She wasn't going to run after him.

8

Tom Woodcock heard the bawling long before he reached the forge. It did not cause him to quicken his step; rather it had the reverse effect. It was the cry of a child on the receiving end of some well-deserved chastisement rather than a signal of danger. Probably young Ned Makepeace, up to his tricks again. No need to get involved, then. Let his father deal with it.

Margery Makepeace stood in the doorway of the forge, arms akimbo. 'That child is good for neither man nor beast!' she declared, her bosom heaving. 'If I've told him once I've told him a dozen times, thou shalt not steal! That's a commandment, isn't it? Well, then, let him do as he's told, but does he listen? He does not! That loaf of bread was no sooner out of the oven and left to cool when he had the heel broken off and stuffed into his mouth. I can't be doing with it, husband. If you don't take him in hand I won't be responsible for what I may do, and that's a fact.'

'Go back to the house, sweeting, and leave all to me.' Adam spoke gently to his wife, who was working herself into hysteria.

Margery gave one vicious look at Meg, who had come to see what all the hullabaloo was about, and flounced away. Adam and Ben exchanged glances.

'She's right, you know, son! That boy has got to learn. You know what Scripture says; *spare the rod and spoil the child*, and young Ned is halfway to being spoiled now. He's almost six years old. High time he started work here instead of idling his days away, getting into mischief. What do you have to say, child? Stealing is a sin and a crime. You should know that by now!'

'I was hungry, Grandad!' the child said sullenly.

'You'll know what hunger means

before this day is out!' Adam told him. 'It's nowt but dry bread for you these next few days, and not the new baking, either. What's left of it,' he added.

Tom appeared in the doorway, grinning. 'Do I smell trouble? Want me to take someone to the lockup, do you?'

Ned gave a cry of horror and bolted. Adam shook his head, smiling. 'Margery caught him filching food. A new loaf, fresh out of the oven, if you please!'

'Ah, well, it's not as if he hasn't done anything that every boy has done in his time. Scrumping apples, new peas straight off the vine, that sort of thing. Not that he can be let off, of course. I'd have thought your wife would have boxed his ears for him and let it go at that.'

'Ah, but that's not all, is it? She wants her own boy taken on here as an apprentice, and we've said no. It's Ned's place by rights, but he refuses all thought of it. Mind you, Dad and I have talked it over, and at the moment we doubt he has the makings of a good blacksmith. He's dead scared of horses and all the whippings in the world won't cure that. I don't know where he gets that from, Tom. Makepeaces have been blacksmiths here since time out of mind, and never a one of them afeared of the trade!'

'Perhaps his mother was frightened by a maddened horse while she was carrying the boy,' Tom suggested, scratching his ear thoughtfully.

'Hulloo there!' Amos Denton now appeared, tugging his forelock in a gesture of respect to Meg, who was still holding up the door post, reluctant to return to the house to brave Margery's fit of temper.

'Morning, Amos!'

'Morning, Constable! Not got hold of the murderer, then, I see. Or have you come to arrest Ben, here?' He laughed at his own wit, displaying several rotting teeth.

'Seen any more strangers about the place, Amos?'

108

'Yes and no.'

'And what's that supposed to mean?'

'Just Mistress Porter's married daughter, home for a visit from Biggleswade, and not before time, either. I heard from Father Wagstaffe's serving woman that the widow's on her last legs.'

'If Meppershall was a bigger place they'd appoint you town crier,' Ben chuckled, but something struck a chord in Meg's mind.

'Mistress Porter? Who's she?'

'That poor old soul who lives in that cottage on the edge of the wood,' Tom told her. 'Come to think of it, she was the only person for miles around who didn't come to take a look at the corpse. She was too sick to rise from her bed, as the priest could testify. I went to call on her later, just for the sake of telling the sheriff I'd questioned everyone, in case he should ask, but it was a waste of time. The woman could barely lift a hand to mop her brow, never mind swinging a scythe.'

'You never spoke to the daughter,

though, I'll be bound!'

'No, Amos, I did not, for the girl was nowhere near Meppershall, either then, or when the crime was committed. Widow Porter said she hadn't seen her for more than two months, and the priest said she'd better be sent for before it was too late, if they wanted to see each other again in this life.'

'Tee hee! D'you call that a girl? She must be thirty-five if she's a day!'

'I was going to tell you the other day, when John Dilley was here, only you sent me packing and I didn't get the chance.' Meg couldn't resist giving Tom a verbal dig. 'I found Mistress Sykes at the stranger's grave, right before Dilley arrived at the church. She said she was praying for his soul, but it seemed odd to me.'

'Goul!' Ben sniffed. 'If he'd died like a Christian nobody would bother to come near him, never mind praying, but being murdered he's a nine days' wonder.'

Tom looked thoughtful. 'Sykes, you

110

say. Now that's a strange one! She's the widow Porter's closest neighbour.' They all looked at him expectantly, but apparently he decided that no connection could be made and nothing more was said.

They were interrupted by the arrival of a florid ploughman, leading a patient shire horse, and Amos reluctantly went on his way. Tom followed Meg as she headed for the house, catching her by the sleeve as she pretended not to notice him.

'I was wondering,' he began humbly, 'if you'd care to come a-walking after church on Sunday.'

'It might rain,' she told him, trying to hide a smile.

'And it might snow in August, or we could all be dead come Saturday! But if tis a fine day on Sunday, what do you say?'

'I shall have to see.'

'Better not leave it too long to decide, then, or I might take some other girl.'

'Please yourself, Tom Woodcock. It

makes no odds to me!'

Meg disappeared inside the house, leaving him standing in the wet grass with his mouth hanging open. Then he brightened. She hadn't actually said no, had she? There was hope for him yet.

Amos toddled off, well pleased with himself. If he'd made trouble for the widow Porter and her stuck-up daughter, it was no more than they deserved. He'd been the village cobbler until his rheumatics got too bad for him to spend long hours bending over the last, and he'd done good work all those years, if he did say it himself. That is, until the Porter woman had brought her old shoes to be mended.

There wasn't much left of them, if the truth be told, but he'd done his best, knowing she probably couldn't afford to buy new. Then she'd refused to pay, saying he'd done shoddy work! If she'd come clean with him and confessed she was unable to pay, he could have accepted that, and let the work go unpaid, out of Christian charity.

What he could not forgive was the fact that she'd berated him in front of a queue of customers, ruining his reputation. Well, she hadn't had a day's luck since. Her one ewe lamb had married a foreigner and trundled off to Biggleswade, and the mother was left alone to struggle on in a penniless old age. Amos himself was alone in the world but he managed to muddle on, having prudently put a bit by over the years.

Where to go next? It was too early to go back to his cottage for a bite of dinner. Might as well go up to the church and call on the priest. Father Wagstaffe might offer to give him a small pot of honey from his own bees, and that would go down a treat.

By the time he reached the church-yard he was feeling winded. Better not arrive at the priest's house all breathless. Besides, he needed to think up some excuse for coming there. He could hardly say he'd come hoping to get a present of honey! The priest was a generous enough man when the fit took him, but he didn't like being taken for granted. Amos leaned on the wall and ruminated.

His eyes widened in surprise when he saw someone coming whom he recognised. He opened his mouth to make one of his harmless jokes. The blow took him by surprise. He had barely a moment to realise what was happening before he fell to the ground. Another blow struck him, and then another.

Father Wagstaffe, returning home, had just released his old horse into the garth and was walking towards his house, when he saw the crumpled form of his elderly parishioner lying on the ground. Apoplexy, perhaps?

He hurried over to render what assistance he could, but Amos was beyond all human aid. Murmuring the appropriate prayers, the priest was unhappily aware that the murderer had struck again.

The murder of Amos Denton hit

people hard. Unlike the previous victim he was one of their own or nearly so. The tragedy left them shocked and fearful.

'I remember when he first came here,' Ben Makepeace said, to anyone who would listen. 'Just past his time as a journeyman, far as I know. He set up in that same little cottage where he's lived up to now, and practiced his trade in that tumbledown little workshop at the back.'

'Where was he from, Dad? I don't think I ever heard.'

'That was before you were born, Adam, or even thought of. Somewhere out of the shire, I reckon. Poor old gaffer! He was always meaning to tidy that place up but he never got around to it. Well, he won't be doing it now.'

'Do you know if he had any relations?' Tom asked. 'Somebody we should notify, perhaps?'

Ben shook his head. 'Nobody that I know of. He never married, and although he did speak of his old mother, back in the days when I first knew him, why, she'll be gone to her reward long ago.'

'Nobody left, then. That's a pity.'

'Oh, it's not so bad,' Ben soothed. 'Old Amos was well thought of. There'll be plenty from hereabouts to follow him to his grave. He won't travel alone to his long rest.'

'That wasn't what I was thinking of, exactly. Sometimes when there's a murder the victim's family can shed light on what provoked the attack. There could be something in old Amos's past that caught up with him, d'you see?'

Swallowing the urge to ask his friend just how many murders he'd investigated in the past — the answer being, none — Adam shook his head.

'I shouldn't think old Amos had anything to hide, or we'd known about it by now, surely? As Dad says, he's been in Meppershall since he was a young man, spending all his time repairing people's boots and shoes. No secrets there! Besides, this is the second death, don't you forget. All this must spring from something entirely different.'

'No need to remind me, Adam Makepeace!' Tom was nettled by the blacksmith's suggestion that he needed his nose pointing in the right direction. 'I have to cover the whole ground, that's all. Leave no stone unturned, as they say.'

Meg had been listening to this exchange, and she spoke up now.

'How was Amos killed, Tom?'

'It was not a scythe this time,' he said, guessing what was going through her mind. 'Something heavy, like a club, I'd say. And the murderer came up behind him and took him unawares. It must have been all over very quickly. The poor old gaffer wouldn't have known what hit him.'

'No sign of the weapon, then?' Adam wondered.

'No, and I don't know where to start looking. It might be anything. Heavy enough to do damage, but light enough for a person to carry about with him without drawing attention to himself.'

'Him? You're sure it was a man, then?'

Tom frowned. 'I suppose it might be a woman, if she was tall. By the look of the wounds on the corpse's head it had to be someone with a long reach.'

'Amos was a shortish man.'

'He was, that.'

Ben glanced around the forge, with its array of instruments used in his trade.

'Any of this lot could dispatch a man fast enough, if one of us was minded to commit murder,' he remarked.

'Nothing like this was used to kill old Amos,' Tom told him. 'I can say that with surety because wood splinters were found in his head.'

With a cry, Meg fled outside, with a hand over her mouth.

'There, now see what you've done!' Adam scolded. 'Have you no sense? Between the pair of you, you've upset poor Meg, and she's not yet over the shock of finding the first corpse!'

'Stuff and nonsense, boy!' Ben dismissed this out of hand. 'If she hears no worse than that in her life, she'll do well! And if she didn't hear it from us someone else would tell the tale. Every detail must be round the whole shire by now.'

'Not quite, Ben, but certainly everyone I've spoken to seems to know as much as I do!'

Speculation was rife. The maids in the Makepeace household were filled with delighted dread, convinced that the killer was lurking nearby, getting ready to pounce on new prey. The younger girl refused to go out alone to peg out the washing, and when Margery refused to let the other go with her, she flew into hysterics, shrieking that they would all be murdered in their beds.

'Make up your silly mind, girl! Get out there with that basket or you'll feel the weight of my hand! Ned can go with you. Unless though he is, the killer won't strike while the boy's on hand as witness. Besides, what makes you think the killer is hanging around here? He'll be long gone, whoever he may be.'

Meg wasn't so sure. Two men had been murdered within a week. Surely there hadn't been two different killers on the loose? If whoever had committed the crimes had remained among them for the intervening days, then it must be someone they knew — a horrid thought! If a stranger was involved, he must have returned, but to what purpose?

Amos Denton had been a nosy old man and a blabbermouth; had he seen something which, if known, could be of vital importance to the murderer?

For once it seemed that Margery felt disinclined to give her full attention to the work of the household. 'I doubt me that Tom Woodcock will get to the bottom of either crime,' she stated bluntly, cautiously lowering herself to the bench which was drawn up to the kitchen table. She nodded her head three times as if to give weight to what she was thinking.

'Why's that, then?' Meg felt irritated on Tom's behalf. He was good enough at his job. It wasn't his fault if the malefactor had been careful to leave no traces of his evil exploits for the constable to find.

'Because he's looking in the wrong places.'

'Is he?'

Margery nodded again. 'The answer lies at Court, you see. And if he were to go there in search of information he'd be none the wiser, and if he takes my advice he'll stay well out of it, or he could find himself in peril. There's some plot afoot, my girl, even treason, mebbe.'

'What on earth are you talking about, Margery?'

Normally mild-mannered, and in any case well used to keeping a curb on her tongue when it came to dealings with her sister-in-law, Meg blurted this out without a second thought. Was the woman mad? Something must have addled her wits, with this foolish talk of plots and treason.

'Perhaps you've forgotten what we heard from the Pastons,' Margery replied, in a tone of voice which suggested that only an idiot could have let it slip out of mind. 'The king has sent his wife away, and by hook or by crook he means to marry that Bullen harlot.'

'I know, but . . .'

'There are people in England — true Catholics, for a start — who are not going to let that happen. It won't surprise me at all if there's an uprising before long, in support of poor Queen Catherine. Never mind the menfolk; the women won't want to see her cast aside like an old shoe, just because King Henry fancies a pretty young thing and wants to take her to his bed.'

'I can't see many women putting on armour and going off to fight, Margery.'

'I'm not saying that, you fool! They'll get behind their husbands and force them to do what's right, and what man will dare to tell his wife he supports the king? That's as good as saying he believes in a man's right to abandon his wife when she's old and lost her looks.'

'I suppose you're right.'

'Of course I'm right! And it's not just the principle of the thing. If they put the queen in a convent she'll be well taken care of, what with the dowry he'll be forced to give her. But what about the rest of us, hey? We can't all go into a nunnery, and how are we supposed to live if our husbands bar the door against us and we no longer have a groat to bless ourselves with?'

'I know all that, Margery, but I still don't see what that has to do with the price of eggs! What about that man I found, lying dead in the churchyard? We're no nearer to learning who he was, or why he was killed.'

Margery was exasperated. 'Why does nobody ever listen to me? That's what I'm trying to tell you. It's my belief he was involved in this business of the king's marriage. Let's say he was a secret messenger, sent to rally the people to the queen's standard. Some enemy, one of the Boleyn faction, mebbe, followed him here and put him to death. What do you think of that?'

She slapped her hands on the table triumphantly.

9

John Dilley was back. He had come riding into the hamlet early in the morning and, apparently with no errand in mind, had stopped at the forge.

'Can I help you?' Adam stepped forward, adjusting his leather apron as he came.

'Er, I was just passing,' the man smiled, tugging his ear.

'And you thought you'd just bide here for a while, to rest the horse,' Adam nodded.

Dilley glanced towards the house, but at first there was nothing to be seen except for a young maid, who was emptying a pail of water over the path. Adam's wife then made an appearance, her voice shrill.

'Don't waste that water there, my girl! Haven't I told you a dozen times?

Throw it on the vegetable patch, where it can do some good! But no! Too lazy to walk a few steps, that's what!' She fetched the girl a resounding clip round the ear.

The two men looked away, unperturbed. Children and servants had to be shown what was what. They had to be kept in order or they'd get out of hand.

'I was wondering,' Dilley began, but left his sentence unfinished.

'Yes?'

'Er, I was wondering about the new murder. Have they caught the culprit yet?'

Adam looked at him levelly. 'You'd best ask the constable about that. You should find him in his cottage unless he's already out and about.'

'Yes, yes, I'll do that.' Dilley swung into the saddle and urged his mount into the lane, just as Ben came out of the house and limped towards the forge.

'Don't know as I'll be much use to you today, lad. I've got a bit of the strike. Come on in the night, it did.'

The ailment known as the black-smiths' strike was caused by too much bending over the anvil, when the back muscles seized up. There was not much that Adam could say in response to this; he knew of old that his father was not looking for sympathy, but just stating a fact.

'Funny thing, that,' he remarked.

'What is, boy?' Ben knew that his son was not referring to his back pain.

'Why, that fellow who was just here.'

'The harness maker, was it? I thought so. What did he want, then?'

'Came here all aimless, like. Wanting to know if they've arrested anyone for bumping off old Amos. Seemed to have trouble getting the words out.'

'What's so funny about that? It's the talk of the shire, I daresay.'

Adam wiped his nose on the back of his hand, sniffing. 'Ah, but what if this Dilley's the killer, Dad? Say he's come here trying to find out if anyone's on to him? He didn't seem to have business in the district. Just passing through, he said.'

'Rubbish! We've no more reason to suspect him than anybody else.'

'Can't be too careful, Dad. Anyway, I told him to go and ask Tom Woodcock, if he's so keen to find out what's happening.'

'You did the right thing, son.'

'That's if he goes there,' Adam grunted. 'If he's guilty he may not go near Tom. Or then again, he might, so as to turn suspicion away from himself.'

'Or pigs might fly,' Ben responded. 'Now, are you going to stand here chatting all day, or will we get some work done here?'

John Dilley, meanwhile, was feeling foolish. He had come all this way in the hope of seeing Adam's sister, Meg, but she hadn't made an appearance. Furthermore, he'd stammered and stuttered like any callow youth, instead of coming out with his request to see the girl. Had old Ben been on the premises he might have summoned up the courage, but somehow he'd not been able to tell the girl's brother what was in his mind.

Instead, he'd blurted out the first thing that came into his head, some foolish question about the cobbler's murder! Now he was on his way home again, not only having failed in his quest but probably having planted doubts in the blacksmith's mind as well.

Dilley's cheeks reddened as he recalled the look on the man's face as he'd directed him to go to the constable. That could mean only one thing; Adam Makepeace thought he must be guilty! Why else would he have suggested it? People from miles around were gossiping about the two slayings at Meppershall, so why couldn't Adam have done the same? All it needed was for him to say 'no news yet', and leave it at that.

Now he was in a fine old muddle, and no mistake! Adam was sure to say something to Woodcock, and the constable, wanting to leave no stone unturned, would come after him. He'd have to explain that he had gone to Meppershall, hoping to see Meg Makepeace, but had lost his nerve at the last moment.

Meanwhile, Tom Woodcock was sitting at the table in his cottage, staring into a mug of ale. He was no closer to solving the death or the identity of the unknown man, and now he had Amos Denton's killing on his hands as well. Why had Amos been done away with? Were there two murderers, or one?

Feelings were running high in the district. The first killing was upsetting, but the victim was a stranger. For all they knew he'd been a bad 'un, who deserved to die. The death of Amos Denton was quite different. Not only was he one of their own, but his death was too close to home, in more ways than one. It had people looking over their shoulders, taking good care to bar their doors at night.

All of a sudden he remembered what Meg Makepeace had told him about

Mistress Sykes. Having nothing better to do, he decided to go and have a word with the woman. Praying at a graveside was no crime, yet there was something odd about it. Father Wagstaffe was always telling his flock to pray for the faithful departed, so as to shorten their time in Purgatory, but everybody had enough friends and relations of their own to think about, without saying Aves at a stranger's grave.

It could be that Mistress Sykes was unusually devout and feared for the soul of the unidentified man, for if his demise wasn't known to his kin, or if he had none, who was there to petition Heaven on his behalf? Or, more likely, perhaps she knew who he was!

He found the woman at home, plucking a goose.

'You'll get a fine pillow out of that lot,' he observed, by way of an introduction.

'Hardly that,' she murmured, not stopping her work, 'but I'll keep them by me until they can be added to, and then we shall see.' She looked up at him, bright-eyed. 'I suppose you've heard from Meg Makepeace that I was at the stranger's grave? Tis true; I was there.'

'Why?' he asked, surprised into bluntness.

The woman shrugged. 'I was passing by, and stopped for a moment, that's all. What does it matter?'

Something about her manner hinted that she wasn't telling the truth, or, not quite all. He narrowed his eyes.

'You know who the man is, or was, don't you, Mistress?'

She made no reply but continued to pluck the white feathers.

'In the name of the law, I command you to give me his name.'

This pompous utterance often worked well with minor transgressors, who could be thus frightened into telling him what he wanted to know, the unspoken addition to the words being 'or else'. In this case it had no effect.

'If I knew the man's name, I should

tell you,' she snapped.

'Then why go there to pray for him? Don't you see, Mistress Sykes, until we can discover who the man was, there is little hope of tracking down his killer. If we could only find his place of abode, and go there to speak to his family or neighbours, we would have some clue as to what happened to him here. Did he have enemies, for example. Had he cheated someone in business? Had he accosted someone's wife or daughter? Had he, perhaps, done you an injury?'

Was he mistaken, or did a flicker of alarm appear in those quite lovely eyes? It was gone so quickly that he wondered if he had been mistaken; a trick of the sunlight, perhaps. He knew nothing to make him think her guilty, but he pounced nevertheless.

It was you, Mistress, was it not? What was it the man did to make you kill him, eh? Had he taken you against your will, is that it? Or stolen your money and goods, perhaps? Whatever it was, you vowed to take your revenge. You followed him to the church yard that morning, did you? Or had you arranged to meet him there?

'Murder was in your heart that day. Perhaps he goaded you. You were possessed with fury. You saw the scythe lying there and you swung it, catching him by the throat. Then, horrified by what you had done, you fled, leaving the corpse bleeding where it lay.'

To Tom's amazement, the woman burst out laughing. 'What a wonderful tale! Methinks you have the makings of a playwright, Master Woodcock. And then I went back to the grave to make sure the man I killed was truly dead and buried! No, you must look elsewhere for your murderer, for it is not I. And if you want to know why I went to pray for the poor man, it was because Mistress Porter asked me to. That is all I have to say.'

Tom Woodcock trudged across the lane to Mistress Porter's rundown cottage. It had the appearance of a house where there is no man in residence to attend to small repairs and thus is left to sink back into itself. The gate swung drunkenly on its hinges and the small kitchen garden off to the side showed weeds sprouting up among the remains of last year's vegetables.

Inside, the place was no better, looking all of a piece with its elderly occupant. Dressed in rusty black, Mistress Porter hobbled about with the aid of a home made crutch, glaring at him. Or perhaps her angry look wasn't directed at him in particular, just at life in general.

'Whatcha want this time, Tom Woodcock? Thought you said your piece when you come before, after that first poor chap got hisself killed. Nothing I could tell you then, and nothing I can tell you now. Best be on your way and stop wasting my time.'

By the look of it she had plenty of time to waste, he thought, wrinkling his nose at the smell. If any housework had been done in this place in the past few weeks, his name was Harry Tudor. Well, if she could come out fighting, so could he.

'I want to know why you sent Mistress Sykes to the stranger's grave, Mistress Porter, and I want a straight answer.'

'I never! And if she says I did, she's a liar!'

'Now why would she lie about a thing like that?'

She looked at him belligerently. 'Who knows what makes folk say the things they do? I didn't even know the chap, so what for would I send her to pray over his grave, eh?'

Quick as a flash, Tom took her up on that. 'Who said anything about praying, eh?'

But she was a match for him, and no mistake about it. In any other situation he might have enjoyed sparring with her. 'Why else go to a new grave, then?' she countered.

'What you doing here, Tom Woodcock? You ain't got no call to come bothering a poor widow woman!'

He swung about to find a tall woman hovering in the doorway. She might have been handsome once but now her face wore a dour expression and her hair was turning grey. After a moment's puzzlement it came to him who she was.

'Jane Porter. Is it you?'

'Jane Pargeter to you, if you please!'

He remembered the widow's only surviving child from his young days, when he had been a carefree barefoot boy, running the lanes with his cronies. Some years older than the rest of them, she had married a few years back and gone away from Meppershall. Now, it seemed, she had returned.

'Pargeter, then,' he agreed. 'Moved back to stay, have you?'

'I have not. No law against coming to visit my old mumma, is there?' She pulled back the cloth covering of the basket she was carrying, revealing a raised pie and a loaf of bread. 'No dangerous weapons here, see?'

Was he mistaken, or did a meaningful

look pass between the two women? Determined to get the information he'd come for, he pushed on.

'Your mother's neighbour was seen kneeling at the place where the stranger lies buried. Praying for his soul, she says she was. That's as may be, but when questioned she said that your mother asked her to go there. I've come to find out why.'

Again the warning look flashed between mother and daughter. Mistress Porter licked her lips.

'Mistress Sykes looks in on me once in a while, just to make sure I'm still alive, like. Jane does her best, but it's a fair trudge from home and she's her own work to see to. She can't be coming here every day. Matilda Sykes is a connection of mine; that is, she was second cousin to my husband, God rest his soul. Well, when she comes we get talking, see, and sometimes I says too much. It's a lonely life, sitting here alone, and when someone's here to listen, I ramble on.'

'No harm in that, Mistress.'

'So, like everybody else in these parts, we got talking about them murders. Poor chap, I said. Lying cold in his grave, with nobody to pray for him. Somebody should go and say an Ave or two over him, I might have said. That's not the same as telling Mattie to go and do it, is it? If she took me up on what I said, out of the goodness of her heart, that's not my doing, is it?'

'I suppose not,' Tom sighed. Stubborn old woman! Put her on the rack and she'd probably stick to her tale, now she had her daughter to back her up.

'I don't suppose you have any idea who the dead chap was?' he asked Jane Pargeter, who shrugged.

'How am I supposed to know that? I don't even live in these parts any more to see who comes and goes. And seeing as I wasn't here when he died, and I didn't get a look at him after, he could be King Harry himself for all I know or care.'

139

The old crone cackled, but why she found this amusing Tom had no idea.

'Whatcha bring me, then?' she asked her daughter. 'Hope it's none of them stale cakes like last time. Could hardly get my teeth through them.'

'I've brought you a nice loaf, Mumma, fresh baked this morning.'

Dismissed, Tom left, closing the door behind him. He waited outside for a moment or two, hearing the hum of muted voices, but it seemed there was nothing more to be gained, so he went on his way, fuming. He'd missed something, somewhere, but be blowed if he could puzzle out what it was.

He must learn the identity of the dead man. That is, the first corpse, he corrected himself. Everyone knew Amos Denton, of course. The only mystery there was why he'd had to die. Supposing there was only one murderer, and not two, then it was safe to assume that he was killed because he knew something, or saw something, that he shouldn't. The poor old fellow was known to have had a loose tongue, but what could he have come across that nobody else was aware of? Some fact that the murderer had to suppress at all costs.

Tom thought about the women he had spoken to that day. Three harmless housewives, on the face of it. Matilda Sykes, whose husband was away at sea. Granny Porter, as some spoke of her; crippled with rheumatics and at times hardly able to move. Her daughter, Jane Porter as was; married to a chap in another village, Pargeter by name.

When her daughter had gone, needing to complete the slow trudge back to where she was staying before the day was too far gone, Mistress Porter sat rocking back and forth in her upright chair. She bit a piece off the rabbit pie her daughter had given her, but she chewed on it without registering the taste.

That constable had gone on his way without learning anything from her, but his arrival had rattled her. Of course she knew who the dead man was!

And hadn't he been to this very cottage, early in the morning on the day of his death? Not that she had seen the corpse for herself, being overcome with the ague and having to stay in bed when everybody else from the district was summoned to the church to view the body.

No, it was Mattie Sykes who had gone there with the rest, lying through her teeth when asked if she knew the victim, and then stopping in on her way home to pass on the news to her cousin's widow. The horror of it!

Mistress Porter wished she could rely on Mattie to keep a still tongue in her head, and her friend had assured her that she wouldn't say a word. Blood, however much diluted by degree of relationship, was thicker than water, after all, but the woman was known to fancy a little drop of home brew at times, which fact boded no good.

What in the world had possessed the fool to say that to Tom Woodcock today, about being told to go to the grave. A slip of the tongue, perhaps, in the heat of the moment? Luckily there was no way the constable could dispute the fact that she'd wanted prayers said for the departed, out of Christian charity. Hadn't the priest encouraged them to do so?

She had handed the ring to Mattie, insisting that she should take it to the grave and bury it there, pushing it deep down as far as it would go.

'Somebody might see me, and wonder,' Mattie had argued. 'Why don't I just hurl it in the stream?'

Mistress Porter had shaken her poor head. 'Not safe, girl, not safe. What goes in can come back out. What if the stream dries up some hot summer, like it did back in 1504? What if that ring came to light then, with his name scratched on it?'

Mattie had scoffed at that. 'So what if it should be found, years from now. Where's the harm? What could connect it with any of us?'

'Because of the name,' Mistress Porter pointed out. 'Now, will you do as I say? My rheumatics are so bad I can't get up out of this chair.'

So Mattie had done as she was bidden, and that, for the time being, was that.

10

As things turned out it was Father Wagstaffe who uncovered the first clue to the mystery. The priest was used to finding tearful women in the confessional, but this time the penitent on the other side of the screen had a story to tell that set him wondering.

Some people believed that they were invisible to the priest when they made their confessions and he did nothing to dispel this notion, but knowing his flock so well he had no difficulty in identifying all by their voices or patterns of speech. Thus he was well aware that it was Mistress Sykes who had something on her conscience.

As usual, she rhymed off a litany of minor sins before coming to the point. 'I know who the deader was,' she whispered. His heart gave an uncomfortable thump. Was he listening to a murderess?

'Go on, my daughter,' he said, into the silence.

'That's it, isn't it?' she answered, sounding impatient now. 'I could have told the constable who it was, but I held my peace.'

'And why was that, my daughter?'

'It wasn't my tale to tell, Father.'

'You can at least tell me.'

'Oh, I suppose so. His name was Job Pargeter. A carpenter from Biggleswade.'

Pargeter. Pargeter. The name sounded familiar, but for the moment he couldn't place why this was so. He sighed.

'Say ten Aves for your other sins, and you must go to the constable as soon as you leave here, and tell him what you know.'

'Oh, I couldn't do that. There's others involved, Father.'

'Others who have had a hand in the man's death, no doubt. They must be brought to book, daughter. Tis man's law, and God's.'

'Couldn't you tell the constable, Father?' she pleaded. 'I don't want it getting back to the person that I told on them. I gave my word, you see.'

'You know very well that anything you say to me is under the seal of the confessional.'

'But if I say it's all right for you to tell, surely that will do?'

'I'll think about it,' he grunted, and proceeded to give her absolution.

When she had gone, and he had ascertained that no-one else was waiting, he went back to his house, wondering what was best to do. Woodcock had to be told, of course, but what of Mistress Sykes? Would spreading the knowledge put her in peril? Surely, the person she was shielding would guess that it was she who had spilled the beans.

But before he could do anything with his new-found knowledge, he had a visitor. Father James Ingram was an old friend. They had grown up together in a small village and later entered the seminary together. After being ordained they had gone their separate ways, but their paths still crossed on occasion and the ties which bound them together as old school mates had never been broken.

'James! What do you want here? Passing through and thought to look me up, I'll be bound! Come inside, man! Come in!'

'I've come here for a purpose,' the other priest told him, 'though I'll not deny it's good to see you again, old friend. And yes, if that's ale in that jug, I'll not say no!'

First the preliminaries. Ingram's horse had to be watered, and turned into the garth where Old Brownie greeted him with a whinny. Then they returned to the house, filled the tankards, and got down to business.

For a long time it had been Father Wagstaffe's belief that important events never came singly, but always in twos and threes. Apparently this was to be the case now.

'Still at Bedford, are you?' he asked, eager to catch up on the news.

'Well, no; and that, in a way, is why I'm here. I was recently transferred to Biggleswade.'

'A pleasant village.'

'Indeed. I had reason to go through the registers of my new parish and there I came across a marriage, solemnised some seven years ago, between a man named Job Pargeter and his wife Jane, born Porter.'

Pargeter again! Father Wagstaffe's hand flew to his mouth as he considered the name of the bride.

'Unfortunately I know something of this man, and nothing to his credit! His poor wife was a parishioner of mine at Bedford, and about the time that this wedding was taking place, she had been abandoned by her husband. Not that it was any loss, for she was often seen limping around the town, displaying a black eye or a bruised cheek, but despite all, marriage vows are binding until death, as well you know.'

'Quite so; quite so. But surely the two Job Pargeters cannot be one and the same? You know how it is with these village families; they pass the same Christian names on down through the generations. This is coincidence, merely.'

'I'm afraid not! I made enquiries, naturally and there's no mistake. The fellow is a bigamist, and must be brought to justice. That is why I've come, my friend. Pargeter may have somehow got wind of my discovery, for he's not been seen in Biggleswade for a considerable time. Since his second wife — if you can call her that, poor soul — since she came from Meppershall he may have come to hide out here.'

'Prepare yourself for a shock, James. Pargeter is here in Meppershall, but he lies in an unmarked grave out yonder. I performed the burial rites myself.'

'Dead! By what means?'

Father Wagstaffe recounted the story of the murder. 'And it was just today that I learned the victim's identity,' he concluded. 'I was getting ready to go to the constable when you arrive on my doorstep.'

'This explains much,' his friend told him. 'Perhaps his deception was discovered; by what means I cannot tell. The second wife who, let us hope, married him in all innocence, is beside herself with fury and grief. She comes home to her own family and tells of her disgrace. Her father, or a brother, perhaps, wreaks revenge on the man who was the cause of her shame.'

Father Wagstaffe shook his head. 'As far as I know, any male relative Jane Porter may have had is buried outside, not far from the fellow who has caused her downfall. Her mother lives here but I know of nobody else, other than a certain Mistress Sykes, a distant cousin.' Now the facts fell into place. This morning's penitent must know a great deal more than she was telling!

Tom Woodcock scratched his head. 'I knew there was something wrong at the Porter cottage, but I couldn't quite put my finger on it! What you suggest may well be true, Father Ingram! That Pargeter was killed because his foul deed was discovered! Jane Porter, as we must call her, seeing as she isn't entitled to use Pargeter's name, comes home to tell her mother what has befallen her. The man follows her here, they argue, and she picks up the nearest weapon and kills him in her fury!'

'Or perhaps in self defence,' Father Wagstaffe suggested. 'Bigamy is a serious crime. He may have wished to prevent her talking. For that reason he may even have tried to kill her. She picks up the scythe, meaning to ward him off. She swings it and without meaning it, the fatal blow is struck.'

'She'll hang in the end, however it happened.' Tom grimaced.

Mistress Porter's eyes widened when she saw the three men framed in the doorway of her cottage. 'What do you want now, Tom Woodcock?' she demanded. 'Coming here day after day, bothering a poor old woman. I've said it before and I'll say it again, I know nowt!'

'Sit down, Mistress,' Tom told her, gently enough. 'This is Father Ingram, who's come all the way from Biggleswade, with something to tell us.'

'I know who he is. I've heard about you. You're the new priest up there.'

'We won't beat about the bush, Mistress,' Father Wagstaffe interrupted. 'We know that the dead man was one Job Pargeter, married to your daughter. Furthermore, he has a previous wife, living at Bedford.'

If they had expected an outcry of shock, or denial, they were wrong. She heard them out, stony-faced. But then, why should they be surprised. Jane Porter must have come running to her mother with the whole sorry tale.

'So what should she do but come home to her mother?' Tom continued, taking this idea to its logical conclusion. 'The man Pargeter came after her and they argued. Perhaps he wanted her to go back with him and keep quiet about what he had done. Perhaps he even said he loved her and wanted them to stay together. But no, she wanted none of it, and she struck him down in her rage.'

The old woman's mouth was working as she listened to this. 'It ain't my Jane you want!' she burst out at last. 'She never killed nobody! Twas me, constable, reverend sirs. I killed Job Pargeter, and I'm glad he's dead. He ruined my poor girl and he deserved to die!'

The three men looked at each other and then back to her. They had come to the cottage in the hope that Jane Porter might be hiding here. It had never occurred to them that it was her mother who had killed Pargeter.

'You!' Tom Woodcock said at last, hardly daring to believe his luck. 'You murdered poor Job Pargeter!'

'Poor!' she cried. 'Nothing poor about that lying, scheming hound! Yes, I killed him, and I'm glad I did!'

'He would have come to justice in the end,' Father Wagstaffe said. 'He would have gone to prison for his crime.'

'And much good that would do my poor girl! Branded as a harlot for living in sin with such a man, for who would believe her innocent? No, he had to be put down, like the vermin he was.'

Tom looked Mistress Porter up and down. Frail and bent, she seemed a most unlikely murderess. He said as much. She looked at him with what seemed like pity.

'You young ones are all the same! See an older person and think them useless at tackling anything that needs health and strength! I was young once, and strong as an ox from working in the fields, and I can still summon up the strength when needs be. I'm crippled with the rheumatics, yes, but even so I have my good days and bad days. Yes, I killed Job Pargeter, and let no man say otherwise!'

Tom scratched his head. 'How then did the killing come about? What was the man doing in the graveyard, and how did you happen to find him there?'

'He come here, to this cottage,' she said sullenly. 'My girl left him when she learned what he'd done. Where else should she go in time of trouble, but to her mother? That Job, he worked that out for himself, and come a-looking, 'cept that she wasn't here, was she?'

' 'I'll get it out of you if I have to wring your neck, old woman',' he cries. 'I tells him to go to hell, where he belongs and we has a tussle. He comes off best out of it, seeing as he's half my age and twice my size and I tells him how my Jane has gone up to the church in search of the priest, to confess all and ask what she must do next.'

Mistress Porter glanced at the priest who frowned. He had seen that wide-eyed look of innocence before and always from some sinner bent on pulling the wool over his eyes.

'Is this the truth, daughter? Think carefully before you speak for your soul's sake!'

'Mumma didn't do it! It was me!'

'No, child! All will be well, if only you

bite your tongue, now!'

Jane Porter stood framed in the doorway. Tom Woodcock's jaw dropped.

'What's this, then?'

'It's like I said, Constable. I killed him. I was a respectable woman until I met Job Pargeter and wed him in all good faith. A cruel husband he turned out to be, always finding fault and too quick with his fists, but even so I kept to my marriage vows, right up to the time when I learned what he'd done, wedding me when he was already tied to another wife. I left him as soon as I found out and came away, but that wasn't the end. No, he wasn't about to give up what was his, so he followed me here, telling me to come home and nobody would be the wiser.'

'And that's when I knew we had to get rid of him,' her mother chipped in. 'I feared for my girl's life after that, for was he likely to let her live, when one word from her could tell the world his secret?'

'But surely someone else also knew

about his first wife?' Father Ingram, who had been listening quietly, spoke up now. 'How else did you learn of that? The person who told you was privy to the secret. Besides that, all would have come to light eventually, as indeed it did when I examined the parish registers.'

The priest's question was never answered, because Tom's mind was still focused on what the older woman had just said.

'You said we, Mistress. We had to get rid of him. Now I have it! Both of you were in on it! As you said, your daughter had gone up to the church, looking for Father Wagstaffe. You sent Pargeter after her. They meet in the graveyard and quarrel. She picks up the nearest weapon to hand — Josh Palmer's scythe, and swings it. He falls dead. She runs off before the deed can be discovered.'

In his excitement Tom failed to notice that his accusations were almost word for word what he had said to

Mistress Sykes. Never mind. He had come to the heart of the matter now.

'Gather up what you need, Mistress Porter. The pair of you are coming to the lockup, and there you'll stay until the sheriff can be contacted.'

Tom Woodcock was a kindly man, who forebore to add that, by this time next week, the two of them could be swinging from the gallows tree. Hanging women was a cruel thing, but the law was a cruel master and murder had been done. An eye for an eye, a tooth for a tooth the Scriptures said. There was no doubt that Jane Porter had been grievously wronged but she had killed a man and therefore she must pay the price.

A thought struck him as he prepared to march the two women away, followed by the two priests. 'But why kill Amos Denton, Jane?'

She looked at him surprised. 'Kill Amos? I did no such thing. I always liked the old fool. Why should I wish him harm?'

Now it was Tom's turn to look amazed. He'd known Jane Porter well when they were young and he could have sworn she was telling the truth now. But if she was, then who had sent old Amos to his maker? Was there yet another killer on the loose?

'What did you want to go and say all that for?' Jane demanded, when she and her mother were alone in the small building which served as Meppershall's lockup. It was seldom used except as a place where the occasional drunkard was left to sober up, or to teach youngsters a timely lesson when they'd been caught scrumping apples.

'I wasn't going to let them hang you, my girl, not after what that blackguard done to you! I'm old now; I've had my life. You've years in front of you yet. Let them hang me, I don't care. There's some days I wish I was dead anyway, the pain in my poor old joints is so bad.'

Jane took her mother by the shoulder and shook her. 'You mean to tell me you think I killed Job?'

'But you told the constable you did, right in front of them two priests!'

'That was to save you, you old fool!' Jane sank down on the rickety bench that was the one piece of furniture in the lockup.

'You thought I did him in! That's a fine thing to think about your own mother! I can't deny I felt like murder when that husband of yours shook me like a dog with a rat, but I couldn't have hobbled halfway to the church, never mind swinging that scythe. Well, we're a fine pair, that's all I can say! Both of us confessing to murder to save the other one. And now see how it's going to end! We'll swing together, with all Meppershall coming out to watch and making a holiday of it.'

'Perhaps it may come out right after all, Mumma.' Jane wiped away a tear that was running down her cheek. 'Whoever killed Amos was probably the same person as did for Job. Tom

Woodcock won't give up now. If he can find that one he may be able to wring a confession out of him and they'll let us go.'

'Tom better hurry up, then,' her mother sniffed. 'When the sheriff gets here and decides we're guilty, he'll tell them to get the nooses ready. Won't matter then if Tom gets the real killer then. Too late for us, it'll be.'

Meanwhile, Tom Woodcock was in conference with the two priests. 'It'll be a day or two before the sheriff comes,' he muttered. 'Pr'aps you reverend gentlemen could have a word with the accused and ask them to be more forthcoming. Mistress Porter is from this parish, Father Wagstaffe; she knows you and may say more to you than she will to me.'

'And I'm the priest at Biggleswade now, where Jane Pargeter has been living,' Father Ingram put in, 'so it is my place to offer spiritual consolation to her. But I must remind you that anything she may tell me in

162

confession cannot be passed on to another living soul.'

Tom nodded. The situation seemed hopeless anyway. 'I must be off. The carter is due at any minute and I want to waylay him with a message to take to the sheriff at Bedford.'

The carter's lips parted in a wide grin which showed an uneven set of teeth. 'So you've solved the crime at last!' he chuckled, 'and caught two of them in your net, too. This'll be worth a pint or two in The Feathers tonight, when I have this story to tell! Mind you, I thought all along it was the woman as did it!'

'What woman?' Having delivered his message, Tom was only half listening.

'Why, the woman I dropped off here on the day of the first murder.'

'Jane Porter, you mean?'

The carter shrugged. 'Just a woman, is all I can tell you. She never told me her name. Dropped her off at that cottage, down beyond, I did.'

Tom sighed. It was one more nail in

Jane's coffin. Now there was proof that she had, in fact, been in the vicinity on the day that her husband's murder had taken place.

11

'I will if I like!' Meg said, her eyes dancing with defiance as she faced her brother.

'We don't know enough about the man,' Adam snapped. 'If you must find yourself a sweetheart, there's plenty of chaps to choose from hereabouts, men whose families we know the history of. I don't like the way this Dilley has been turning up round here where there's been two murders right under our noses.'

'Fie! Nothing to do with him, were they? It was the widow Porter and her daughter did that, as everybody knows. That's why Tom's got them safely locked up, waiting for the sheriff to come and sort them out!'

'I suppose Dilley's innocent of that business,' Adam conceded, 'but that doesn't make him good marriage material. If I were you, I'd think twice before stepping out with him!'

'Oh, leave the girl alone,' Ben said peaceably. 'She's past seventeen. Time she was thinking about getting wed. And as for Dilley, he spent too much time dithering while he was trying to pluck up the courage to ask Meg out. That don't sound like one of your bold swains with seduction on his mind. Besides, he has a good trade. There'll always be a need for well-made harness. He'll never lack for work.'

Adam was not convinced. 'Never mind all that. She doesn't know the man, that's what I'm saying.'

'And she won't, either, unless she spends time with him. What harm is there in walking out with a chap? She can always throw him over if she don't like what she sees.'

'Why are you two talking about me as if I wasn't here?' Meg demanded. 'Not that it matters. I mean to do as Dad says, so there!'

The thought of being courted by the

handsome John Dilley was greatly exciting to Meg. All her life she had played second fiddle to the other women in the household, bidden to get on with her work and mind her manners.

Meg told herself that she would not rush into marriage just to get out from under Margery's thumb, but if she did get wed, that would be an added bonus. And it was like Dad said; she was seventeen and it was time to settle down.

She wasn't in love with John yet, but that could come. Meanwhile it was evident that Tom Woodcock also had his eye on her. He hadn't come out and declared himself, but he was always making excuses to be near her, and what about that outing to Bedford? She smiled at the thought of it.

She just might consider Tom if her relationship with John Dilley fell through, but she'd known him all her life, as a friend of her older brothers. She was comfortable with him, but where was the romance? She didn't feel weak at the knees when she saw him coming up the lane, and she had to admit that the harness maker did have that effect on her!

Like now, when she went out to greet him, as he slid down from his horse's back.

'Shall we go walking?' he enquired.

'I don't mind,' she murmured. She was too busy looking at him to come up with a sensible answer at once. He was wearing a dark green doublet with hose of apple green, and his broad brimmed hat had a feather in it, a red one. Now what sort of bird had feathers of that hue? Perhaps it was dyed.

'Or we could ride around the lanes and you could show me the sights,' he suggested.

'That would be nice, but won't your horse be too tired? You have the homeward journey still to make, remember.'

'Not if you invite me to stay for an hour or two after our outing, Meg. The beast can rest then.'

All this, of course, was simply small talk. There was nothing she wanted more than to be out in the countryside, riding pillion behind him, with her arms around his waist. And, by the sound of it, he wished to spend as much time as possible with her!

Meg and her sweetheart were not the only ones on the road that day. The carter was well pleased with the work that had come his way during the past weeks. His livelihood depended on transporting goods and people from one place to another.

Well respected though he was, his trade was an up and down one. 'Feast or famine,' he was sometimes heard to say. He could go for some time without being hired, and that was when funds ran low. Then all of a sudden, everything happened at once. People had goods to send, and they all wanted them delivered yesterday! It was no good saying he was busy, he'd attend to it later. Turn away good work and people went elsewhere, and the next time they remembered how he'd said no before, and would pass him up.

Well, he'd been going through Meppershall, carrying six bolts of cloth for a tailor five miles to the south, when that constable, Tom Woodcock, had come hurrying out to flag him down. He'd been given a coin to take a message to the sheriff, and no doubt he'd get another when it was safely delivered. And there was a good story to go with it. Not one, but two murderesses safe in custody! That should earn him a good few pints of ale in the taverns when he told folk there what he'd heard.

It was a long old haul to Bedford town, and it was late when he arrived back at the house where he lodged. He saw his horse comfortably settled before he went for a meal. Without the animal he would not be able to ply his trade, so he always made sure that the beast was fed and made comfortable for the night before he did anything else.

Could the message wait until morning, perhaps? He reluctantly decided that it could not. Besides, he wanted the reward that delivering it would bring. He trudged along to the lockup where possibly the sheriff would be sitting in the turnkey's dwelling, talking.

'Not here, Steve!' the turnkey told him. 'Missed him by an hour or more, you have.'

'Where's he gone, then? I've brought him a message from the constable at Meppershall. Seems the fellow's solved a murder they had down there the other day. Wants the sheriff to get in on it before the hanging.'

'How'd he manage that, then? Catching the killer, I mean.'

They discussed this pleasurably for some time. At last the carter got up to go.

'That's right. You try The Fox And Goose,' his friend told him. 'He likes to go there of an evening when he's staying in town.'

When the carter arrived at that hostelry the sheriff was nowhere to be seen, but he knew the landlord well and it wasn't long before he was invited to tell his story. Others gathered round and he was soon well away, embroidering the few facts that he knew as he went along.

'May as well have another one,' the landlord encouraged. 'It's only a short while to closing. Sheriff won't call in here now. Try again in the morning.'

The carter needed no second bidding.

It was when the landlord had called time and his patrons were getting up to go, that the carter noticed the woman. She had entered by a side door and at first he thought she was some man's wife come to escort her wayward husband home. But when she crossed in front of him, on her way to the room behind the bar, he saw her face.

'Who's that?' he asked, shaken.

'A widow woman, name of Pargeter. Least ways, they call her a widow, but so far as I know they never did hear what became of him. Disappeared a few years back, leaving her to fend for herself. My wife pays her to do a bit of cleaning here. She comes at night after you lot goes home.'

'Funny, I coulda sworn . . . '

But before he could finish his sentence the landlord's wife came out from the inner room, beckoning her husband and the carter was left alone, scratching his head.

'That ain't no widow Pargeter,' he muttered, as he stumbled the outside door. 'Her name's Porter, ain't it? That's the one I took to Meppershall the day of the murder. And what's she doing in Bedford now, then? Only this morning the sheriff told me she was safe in the lockup.'

There would be no sleep for him now. He would have to traipse round Bedford until he found the sheriff. One good thing; the taverns would all be closed, so he had a better chance of tracking him down.

He went from one inn to another, but there was no sign of the sheriff. Finally one landlord, annoyed at having had to open up after he'd secured all for the night, told him where the man might be found.

'Ask at Anne Wilmot's. She keeps a respectable house and don't charge too much. Careful with his money, sheriff is! Don't worry about poor wretches like us making a living if he can find lodgings a penny cheaper elsewhere! Yes, you try there.'

Jane Porter started up, her eyes full of fear. 'Where are you taking us? It's not the hangman, is it? You can't execute us without a trial!'

'Nobody is going to hang you, mistress, or not today, anyhow. Just do as I ask and come with me and you'll see what it's all about. Can I trust you to come quietly, or do I have to fetch the shackles?'

'We'll come quietly,' Mistress Porter told him. 'I don't want no chains. My rheumatics won't stand for it.'

Tom nodded and stood aside so they could step into the yard. Blinking in the sunshine after having endured two nights and a day in the gloom of the lockup, the two women stared about them. A fine roan mare was tethered to the hitching rail, while nearby, the carter's horse, still between the shafts, waited patiently, his head drooping.

'All set then, master Constable? Can I be on my way?' the carter called.

'You can, if the sheriff is satisfied with the evidence you've given.'

The carter opened his hand to reveal two coins. 'Satisfied enough to pay me for my trouble, sir! Oh, I haven't been paid for giving evidence,' he added quickly, catching a glare from Jane Porter. 'Twasn't a bribe! Twas for bringing the prisoner along, see?'

Tom led the way to his house where several people were already waiting; the sheriff, a woman bound in chains and Father Wagstaffe.

'Sit there,' he directed, pointing to a scuffed wooden bench, before setting himself on an upturned bucket. The only chairs were taken up by the others present. Tom's cottage was no palace but it was infinitely preferable to the dank cell that constituted the lockup and so a more fit place in which to entertain the sheriff.

Mother and daughter glanced at the prisoner and looked away, Jane Porter fixing her gaze on the smoke-darkened ceiling and the widow studying her scuffed shoes.

'Let the enquiry begin,' the sheriff stated. He recited a list of events and dates, while his audience listened in silence. Then he indicated Father Wagstaffe. 'I have asked the good priest to be in attendance as advocate for the prisoners, to speak in their defence, if he can, when necessary.'

'And a good thing, too, widow Porter interrupted. Only the high and the mighty gets lawyers. For the rest of us tis rough justice, all too often!'

'Silence! I am told that the two women here, the widow Porter and her daughter Jane, born Porter but known as Pargeter, stand accused in the death of one Job Pargeter of Biggleswade, who was most cruelly done to death on or about the fifteenth day of May this year.'

'However, Steven Bartlett, carter of Bedford has given evidence that the prisoner, Mistress Mary Ann Pargeter, lawful wife of the said Job Pargeter, was the woman he brought to Meppershall on the day of the murder and whom he set down near the cottage of the widow Porter.'

Tom Woodcock's glance rested on the widow for a long moment. It was impossible to read what she might be thinking, but one thing was certain, the sheriff's remarks had come as no surprise.

'What have you to say to this?' the sheriff asked the prisoner, who shrugged.

'What is there to say? I cannot deny it, since I was there at the time.'

'And how do you plead to the murder of Job Pargeter? Guilty, or not guilty?'

'Oh guilty, I suppose.'

At this, the priest leaned forward in his chair. 'Have a care, Miss Pargeter. Say nothing which could be taken and used against you.'

She shook her head at him. 'I'm so tired, Father. I haven't had a decent night's rest since all this started. I've committed a grievous sin and I know I have to pay, so all I want is to get this over with and have peace at last. When I come to Judgement I hope that Our Saviour will have mercy on me, for He alone knows what I've had to endure these years past.'

Somehow Tom believed that she was sincere in what she said, not like some villains who, being found out, claimed mitigating circumstances, or a new-found belief in God. He, too, was eager to hear the story and was pleased when the sheriff invited the woman to explain what had happened.

'It's all the fault of the king, really,' she began, stopping in confusion when the sheriff glared at her, instructing her to stick to the facts and not to mouth treason to add to her crimes. Taking a deep breath, she began again.

'I was young when I married, good sirs, and thought I had a good husband. I was a good wife, also, except for one thing. I was barren and that was the good Lord's doing, for in His wisdom he chose not to send me children. Job wanted sons, and when I was unable to give him any, he began to beat me, saying it was all my fault.'

'Then one day he did not come home after work. I waited and waited, until a week had passed and still he did not come. By then I knew that something must have happened to him. In some ways I was glad because his temper was so bad that at times I feared for my life.'

'Some years later a friend of mine went to a cousin's wedding at Biggleswade and there among the neighbours who had come to the feast she saw my Job sitting there with a new wife, if you please! Her, there!' She pointed an accusing finger at Jane.

'And she told you what she had seen.'

'I didn't believe her at first. Job didn't know her and she'd only seen him from a distance in the past. But one day I went to Biggleswade and here he was. I waited until he left the house and then I went to see that one and told my story.'

'Is this true?' the sheriff demanded.

Jane nodded. 'I thought she was mazed by the sun until she showed me her wedding ring. Job had one just the same. When we met he told me he was a widower whose wife had died in childbirth, along with their first child. On account of that he used to blame me when I couldn't give him the sons he wanted. Every month when I had to say I'd failed again, he'd beat me without mercy. When we heard that the king meant to put his barren spouse away and take a new wife who would do better, he kept saying that Old Harry had the right idea. Some day he'd do it to me. I thought that was just talk, of course, but when Mistress

Pargeter told me what he'd done, I was so ashamed I just up and left. Back to Meppershall I came, home to Mumma.'

Mary Ann Pargeter took up the story again. 'I didn't go back to Bedford right away. I took lodgings nearby and watched the house. I saw that one leaving with her bundle. She'd told me she meant to come to Meppershall and I believed her. Next I saw him trudging off, without his tools, so I guessed he'd be going after her.'

'Had he a horse?' Tom interrupted, but by way of reply she looked across at Jane, who shook her head.

'Tis not so many miles to Meppershall. He could do that in a day. I waited until morning and then I bespoke a ride with the carter. These two know the rest.' She slumped forward, her chains rattling.

'And he came to your cottage,' Tom told the widow, who nodded.

'Jane had come and gone. I knew the blackguard would come looking for her, so I sent her to Mistress Sykes, knowing she'd hide her until we could decide what to do. Sure enough, in he comes and starts knocking me about, trying to make me tell. That's when his ring fell off, although I didn't notice till later. I couldn't take no more so I told him she'd gone to the priest and off he trots to the church.'

'And just as I was nearing the cottage I saw him coming out,' the prisoner said, 'and running towards the church. He didn't see me at first, but I caught up with him in the graveyard and was he surprised to see me!'

'So you killed him,' the sheriff suggested.

'Not right away! We argued and he said things. Nasty things that got me all riled up. I don't know what came over me. I saw that scythe lying there and I started swinging it about. I only meant to give him a fright, but somehow things went wrong. He went down gurgling and clutching at his throat, all bloody. I was scared then and I ran and ran until I could move no more. I didn't dare start back to Bedford in case there was a hue and cry and I was stopped on the road so I stayed back in the woods, sleeping rough and eating whatever I could find.'

'But why kill Amos Denton, then? That was you, wasn't it?'

She sighed. 'Was that his name? A few days later I came back to the village, thinking I might see the carter and get a ride back home. But I met that man and he stopped me, asking who I was, saying that everybody was keeping an eye open for strangers. 'Heh! Heh!' he laughed. 'Happen I should let the constable know'. Well, I couldn't take that risk, so I walloped him one with an old pike I saw lying in the ditch. I didn't mean to kill him. I just wanted him stunned long enough to make my getaway.'

So that was the story, out in the open at last. Tom shuddered, thinking about what might have happened if Meg had arrived at the churchyard just a few minutes sooner. The sheriff escorted the prisoner back to the lockup, there to await her fate.

'What about us, then?' the widow asked, seeing that her daughter appeared to have been struck dumb.

'You're free to go,' Tom told her, 'though you richly deserve a day in the stocks for leading me up the garden path!' She scowled at him as she limped to the door.

Tom Woodcock approached the smithy, a silly expression on his face. In his hand he held a small posy of meadow flowers, such as a lover might present to his lady. He approached the Makepeace home by way of the forge and stopped in to exchange a few words with father and son.

'I see you got to the bottom of the mystery at last, then,' Adam joked. 'It's a good job that carter had his wits about him, or poor widow Porter might have gone to her doom, and her daughter with her.'

'I pity that Pargeter woman,' Ben remarked. 'The poor soul had a cruel time of it with that brute of a husband. It's no wonder she saw red when she caught up with him in the end.'

'Amos Denton's the one who deserves your pity,' Tom replied. 'His only fault was to be in the wrong place at the wrong time.'

'He always did have a long nose, Tom. I always did say it would be the undoing of him in the end and now I'm proved right.'

'So you did, Dad,' Adam agreed. 'What I don't understand is how Jane Porter got entangled with that Pargeter chap in the first place. Do you know, Tom?'

'As it happens, I do. Now they're out of danger the widow Porter is blabbing to anyone who'll listen to her. It seems she used to have a sister who lived in Biggleswade where this Pargeter worked at times. The woman had a growth and there was nothing the apothecaries could do for her. She lingered for a long time, suffering terribly and Jane went there to look after her.

'Apparently Pargeter came to the house to do work of some sort and that's where he came across Jane. He paid court to her, presenting himself as a single man and when the aunt died and Jane was all set to return to Meppershall, he prevailed upon her to marry him.

'He seemed like an upstanding chap and the widow was pleased to see her daughter wed at last for she was past her prime. It took place in the local church there, all above board, as was thought at the time, but after a while it all turned sour. As I see it the man must have been half touched to do what he did and more than foolish to think of using what the king is getting up to with his paramour as an excuse.'

'My wife wants to know what they'll call it if the king marries Nan Bullen while poor Queen Catherine is still alive,' Adam mused. 'Will that be bigamy like Pargeter did, or does the Pope really have the authority to call it a marriage that never was?'

'Let's leave that to the clergy,' Ben put in. 'We've had enough talk of death and sin of late. We've had good news here, Tom, and much to celebrate!'

'What's that, then?'

'For one thing, Margery is enceinte. A few months from now Adam will have another son!'

'Or a daughter.' Adam grinned. 'Unlike the king, we don't mind either one. We've time to spare for a whole quiverful of young uns yet!'

'And our Meg is getting wed,' Ben went on. 'John Dilley's proposed and she's accepted him. What do you think of that, eh?'

'I hope she'll be very happy,' Tom managed to say. Unseen by his two friends he let the pretty posy fall to the ground behind him where he crushed it with his heel.

And although his heart was broken, he truly hoped she'd find all the happiness in the world with her handsome harness maker, for he could never wish her otherwise.

Other titles in the
Linford Romance Library:

ENCORE FOR A DREAM

Sheila Lewis

Limelight Theatre, struggling to survive, is temporarily saved when three sisters unexpectedly inherit it. Rosalind, Olivia and Beatrice are captivated by its charm and the loyalty of the company. With no theatrical experience, the girls strive to combine their own careers with working at Limelight — especially with Gil, the dedicated theatre director. However, an ongoing shortage of cash, a disastrous storm and unforseen tragedy threatens everyone's livelihood, while the girls also have to deal with personal emotional turmoil . . .

REAP THE WHIRLWIND

Wendy Kremer

Briana, passionate about environmental protection, is visiting Turtle Island in the Caribbean. When she discovers Phoebe, the elderly owner of the island, is considering selling it to Nick, Briana is concerned that he'd exploit the island. Determined to prevent this, she attempts to establish 'friendly tourism' there instead, although Nick is extremely sceptical. In reality he doesn't want to change a thing — but certainly relishes a fight. But when Phoebe has a heart attack, he blames Briana's new scheme . . .